Bae Belongs to Me

Aryanna

Lock Down Publications & Ca$h Presents
Bae Belongs to Me
By Aryanna

Aryanna

Lock Down Publications
P.O. Box 1482
Pine Lake, Ga 30072-1482

Visit our website at **www.lockdownpublications.com**

First Edition April 2017
Printed in the United States of America
This is a work of fiction. Names, characters, places, and incidents either are products of the author's imagination or are used fictitiously. Any similarity to actual events or locales or persons, living or dead, is entirely coincidental.

Cover design and layout by: Dynasty's Cover Me
Book interior design by: Shawn Walker
Edited by: Lauren Burton

Stay Connected with Us!

Text **LOCKDOWN** to 22828 to stay up-to-date with new releases, sneak peaks, contests and more...

Thank you!

Submission Guideline.

Submit the first three chapters of your completed manuscript to ldpsubmissions@gmail.com, subject line: Your book's title. The manuscript must be in a .doc file and sent as an attachment. Document should be in Times New Roman, double spaced and in size 12 font. Also, provide your synopsis and full contact information. If sending multiple submissions, they must each be in a separate email.

Have a story but no way to send it electronically? You can still submit to LDP/Ca$h Presents. Send in the first three chapters, written or typed, of your completed manuscript to:

LDP: Submissions Dept
Po Box 1482
Pine Lake, Ga 30072

DO NOT send original manuscript. Must be a duplicate.

Provide your synopsis and a cover letter containing your full contact information.

Thanks for considering LDP and Ca$h Presents.

Acknowledgements

I'm gonna keep this short and sweet. I got to thank
God, my family, my fans, my friends, my label and last
but not least my haters. I appreciate all the contribu-
tions one way or the other.

Dedication

This book is dedicated to all the crazy bitches that hide
it well.

Aryanna

Chapter 1

Ahmani

The perpetual frown that had been on my face for months – ever since I got locked up and charged with multiple bodies – somewhat evaporated as I sat down at the table next to this old head named Doug and re-read the sweet-scented letter I had received yesterday. The words played like a soft melody in a nigga's ear.

I saw you again today, and I gotta admit you're sexy, even though you don't smile. I know I'm not in your situation, and I understand you have nothing to smile about, but I still can't help wondering how you will look if you do. Your skin looks so soft, and I imagine it tasting like dark chocolate on my tongue. Your strong jawline and chiseled features make you breathtakingly handsome and masculine, but your eyes tell me you would be gentle with me in every way that counted. I can't lie though, I've envisioned how your big, rough hands would feel against the softness of my skin, or wrapped in my hair as you did unspeakable things to me. Just writing you about my thoughts has me wet all over again, but I know just the trick to relieve this tension. Maybe in my next letter I'll be able to describe it to you step-by-step. For now, I just wanted to give you something to think about, and to let you know you're being thought of. Keep your head up and maintain. I'll be waiting for you.

I shook my head in mild amusement and passed the letter to Doug. "Ay, unc, read this shit. It's from that mystery chick again."

He took the letter from me and read it. Passing it back to me, he remarked, "Damn, my nigga, she talkin' a good game."

"I know, right? But I don't even know this broad. I've gotten a letter every week for the last month, but there's never a return address, and she ain't signed her name once," I replied, frustrated, yet intrigued.

"Well, obviously she's a fan. Think about it, youngin'. She prolly saw you on the news. Shit, you should get her to send you some flicks so you can see how she look."

"A fan? Bruh, if a bitch is a fan of a nigga facing three bodies, then she's got more issues than me! I've heard of them chicks who send all types of love letters and marriage proposals to serial killers and shit, and I can't deal with no parts of that kinda crazy," I said, shaking my head.

"Real talk: beggars can't be choosy, my nigga. If you don't get from under these murder charges, you looking at forever and some change. I know you ain't got more than some breaking and entering and burglary charges on your record, but this time there's some dead white folks. And you know like I know, these racist-ass people are gonna be looking for a hanging tree. If this broad wanna rock with you, then let her, because once that gavel bangs, a lot of muthafuckas is gonna forget you."

His words rang with truth, even though they were hard to digest. Old man Doug was a veteran of the system and doing time, so there was no doubt he knew what the deal was. It was for that reason I came to him for advice and guidance, despite how taboo it was to discuss your case in the county jail. I was 20 years old with plenty of street smarts, but old man Doug was in his fifties and knew more about being on the wrong side of the judicial system than anyone I'd run across. That didn't mean I trusted him, because the streets taught me to trust no one, but I felt like I could give him the benefit of the doubt after being around him for the last six weeks.

In all honesty he'd helped me keep my sanity, because being locked up in the Prince William County Jail facing murder charges took a lot out of a nigga. The state of Virginia was the wrong place to kill someone, especially if you were black and the victim was white.

All I knew at this point was I was being accused of crimes I didn't commit. Was I guilty of being a hustla and sometimes thief? Absolutely, but that was a long way from dropping the hammer on two people and making a third disappear. I wasn't about that life.

"I hear what you're saying, pops, but you know like I do I've got more important shit to occupy my mind with," I said, taking the letter from him and putting it back in the envelope.

"You ain't never lied, but it's good to relax your mind every now and again. Besides, if she looks as good as she talks, then thoughts of her can keep you company during those long and lonely nights. Think about it," he advised, getting up from the table and going back to his cell.

I was sure I would think about it, but I didn't want to. Not because I wasn't moved by attractive women, because I was, and I loved pussy as much as the next man, but I didn't wanna think about how many long, lonely nights loomed in my future. The entirety of my criminal life had been about survival, not getting rich, so never did I see myself in this situation, looking at six hundred years. I mean, who gives a muthafucka six hundred years? In the state of Virginia, that's what a life sentence added up to, and according to my public defender, what I was looking at.

"Ahmani Monroe!"

Turning toward the front door of the pod, I saw a deputy standing there with more mail in his hand, looking in my direction. I walked over to him and received my second letter of the day, but this one wasn't fan mail. It had the seal of the Prince William County Courts on it. I quickly made my way back to my cell, relieved my cellmate wasn't inside so I'd have a few moments of privacy to read about my legal situation. It was hard enough to keep shit under wraps when you were forced to share a cell with at least one extra person, so when it came to my legal mail I liked to read it A.S.A.P. and mail it home to my mother for safe keeping.

Opening the letter, I scanned the few typed lines, feeling a little relief my situation might finally be improving somewhat. Everybody knew public defenders weren't shit on a good day, but somehow I'd managed to be saddled with the worst of the worst. In the month and a half I'd been locked up, the only time I'd seen the dude was when I'd been arraigned and when I'd gone up for a bond hearing once my third warrant for murder was served. There was no way I could go to war with a lawyer who wasn't motivated, so I'd asked to change counsel. I'd even gone so far as to write letters to lawyers who did pro bono work for the public defender's office, and the proof of my hard work was in my hands.

I peeked out my cell door to see if anyone was on the phone, and seeing an open jack had me on the move to grab it before someone else did. Some niggas could spend all day on the phone, but I only had one person to call, one person who cared enough to answer. As the phone rang in my ear, I was beginning to worry I wouldn't get the answer I was looking for this evening, but suddenly I heard her voice.

"Hey, Mom, what's going on?"

"Nothing, just tired, baby. How you holdin' up in there?"

I loved talking to my mom, but I hated that question because I knew how much she worried. I wasn't her only child, I had a younger brother and sister, but I was her firstborn and according to her I was hardheaded, just like my daddy. Whoever the hell he was. It didn't matter that I was six foot, two-and-a-half inches and 250 pounds of solid muscle, or that my fight game was phenomenal, because all she saw was her baby and she worried.

"I'm okay, Mom. I'm actually calling to give you some good news. I just got a letter from the courts telling me I've got a new lawyer. His name is Michael Sprano," I said, reading from the letter in my hand.

"That's great, sweetheart! Maybe now you'll have someone who gives a fuck about the fact you're innocent in all this."

I wasn't purely innocent but I damn sure wasn't a murderer. "Yeah, Mom. I mean, you know I didn't kill anybody." I whispered, looking around to see if anyone was listening to my conversation.

Everyone in the jail knew why I was here, and the first thing I'd learned from old man Doug was snakes were lurking. A lot of people would love to try to go to the prosecutor with their lies about how I'd told them I'd killed the Hudson family, hoping to cut a deal for themselves. I'd accepted the fact this would undoubtedly happen, but I wasn't about to help these thirsty-ass niggas out by allowing them to pick up seeds from my convos.

"I know you didn't kill anyone, Ahmani. I raised you better than that. I may not approve of your life choices, with how you take care of yourself, but I never judged you, either. I grew up in the same rundown houses in Georgetown South I raised you in, so I understand your mentality to survive and take care of yourself. There is nothing in you that could convince me you stabbed that man and woman, and did God-knows-what with their daughter."

Her words gave me comfort. I came from the slums where some mothers didn't give a damn about their children, so her belief in me actually meant something because it wasn't a given. It would've been easier for her to turn her back on me, especially with my face being plastered all over the news on a regular basis. She wouldn't take the easy way out, though. I was Tamika Monroe's son, and she didn't give a fuck who knew it.

"Hopefully this new lawyer will help prove my innocence, Mom, because I really wanna come home. How are Kendrick and Keisha?"

"They're good. You know they're too young to really understand what's going on," she replied softly.

I prayed she was right and the innocence of my twin five-year-old siblings was intact. I never wanted my bullshit to rub off on them. It had seemed like a crazy move when my mom had first told me she was pregnant six years ago, but I could tell she was a different person than the mother who'd raised me. By then I was already more-or-less on my own, and she'd found a way to get her shit together so she could move out of the ghettos of Manassas, Virginia. It wasn't like she was living in the white people's neighborhood now, but the townhouse she and my siblings shared was nice. They would have it better than me, and part of making sure of that was keeping them in the dark about my legal troubles.

"Have they been going to school?" I asked.

"You know I'm not letting them miss a day, and I'm getting daily reports from their teacher to make sure nobody is fucking with them."

"That's good, Momma. Listen, I want you to write this lawyer's number down so you can call him in the morning and find out how serious he is about defending me."

"Hold on while I get something to take the number down with," she replied.

Even though I was only in the county jail, using the phone still required constant observation, especially given the fact I was fitted with a red wristband signifying the seriousness of my crime and I was housed with likeminded individuals. For this reason, I never had my back to the inmates moving around the pod. Instead I kept my back on the wall next to the phone where I could see everything. Looking around now, I saw dudes lining up at the door, which meant it was 7:00 p.m. and the nurse was coming through.

That also meant the late-night phone bonin' was getting ready to start for the niggas who called their girls back to back until 9:00 p.m. lockdowns. My first day in here I'd seen a muthafucka get the white meat in his forehead exposed over the phone, and that was lesson enough for me on how serious fucking with a nigga's phone time was.

"Okay, baby, give me the number," my mom said, coming back to the phone.

I ran off his name and number really quickly and told her I'd call her again tomorrow, but before I could hang up she hit me with a surprise.

"When I got home today there was a message for you on the answering machine."

"Oh yeah? From who?" I asked, more than a little confused as to why anyone would leave a message for me at my mom's. Everyone knew I didn't live there, and I barely even crossed her threshold when invited.

"She didn't leave her name. She just said she was a friend and she wanted to offer her support because she knew you were innocent."

"That sounds weird," I replied slowly.

"Not when you think about it. I mean, anyone who knows you knows you're incapable of cold-blooded murder."

"I guess. Did she say anything else?" I asked.

"She left her number, which was (571) 251... She said you'd know her because she's a fan."

Chapter Two

After six weeks, I knew all too well it was a ridiculous waste of time to look for any comfort in the plastic mats that stood between me and the concrete slab I was lying on. Still, I was doing more tossing and turning on this night than usual, and I had a sneaky suspicion it had to do with the phone number still tucked into my sock. Part of me had wanted to immediately call it as soon as I'd hung up with my mom, but the other part of me was glad someone else had the phone next because I needed time to think. There was no name attached to that phone number, but I had a feeling the female on the other end was the same one who'd been writing me. What did she want, though?

Was she some lonely housewife or some ugly fat chick looking for any attention she could get? I had way too many questions without answers, which was why I was lying flat on my back looking at the ceiling, listening to my cellmate rattle the walls with his snoring. I was tempted to punch him in his shit, but I was hoping maybe the rhythmic noise would lull me to sleep.

While I waited on sleep, my mind kept going back to this mystery woman. I wasn't no pretty nigga, but I was used to getting attention from females because I had a certain swag about me. It did help that I had nice, white teeth and an easy smile, not to mention the light brown eyes in contrast to my dark complexion.

Still, I'd never had a woman come at me on some secret admirer type shit before. It was flattering, but weird, and I made a concerted effort never to trust weird shit because it only led to bad things. I should've just put the number, the letters, and whomever was behind them completely out of my thoughts and focused on how to get out of my current mess. So why couldn't I do that?

If I was being real with myself, I knew it was because I was lonely and still heartbroken from my breakup with Elyse. Even though I was smart enough to see what we had was nothing more than puppy love, it still hurt when the one you claimed as wifey turned out to be a ho.

I wasn't the type to go at no dude behind his decision to follow his dick, because his dick didn't owe me loyalty. Instead I went to Elyse on some real nigga shit and asked her to keep it one-hundred for the sake of everything we'd been to each other. We'd met as juniors in high school when she moved to Manassas three years ago, and our connection was instant. I mean, she was a bad bitch, standing five feet, eleven inches with a well-proportioned 185 pounds of juicy curves. With a beautiful cocoa-butter complexion, light gray eyes and long brown hair, she was definitely turning heads in a hurry.

She got my attention on the first day, but she only kept it because she was smart, and I respected that more than her beauty. I tried to ignore the warning bells and questions of longevity when I smashed two days after we met, figuring our connection was just that deep. It took me three years to figure out Elyse just loved sex, and when she wasn't fucking me she was letting some other nigga run up in her. It hurt, but I hid it well. There was no one to hide it from at this moment, though, so I could acknowledge the pain and the truth that it was affecting my ability to walk away from this new chick.

I wanted to and needed to get over Elyse, and maybe this mystery woman could help with that. Then again, maybe that was too much to hope for and I should just be alone.

A high note in my cellmate's snoring punctuated the fact I wouldn't be alone for a long time, which only added to my frustration. Reaching under my mat, I grabbed my homemade earplugs and pushed one into each ear. They were made out of the flip-flops we were given to take a shower with, and they didn't completely drown out all the noise, but that wasn't a bad thing. When you were locked up, you never really slept. You just rested because you never knew when shit was gonna kick off. So, the last thing you'd ever wanna do is completely dull your most valuable sense, because hearing was definitely the difference between life and death.

With my earplugs in, the howling was reduced to a dull roar, but I was at least able to turn my mind away from kicking that nigga's teeth down his throat. The argument within about whether to call my mystery woman or not continued going in full force for what seemed like forever until I lost track of it in the blurred lines of sleep.

If I was under oath, I would've sworn my eyes were only closed for a moment, but when I opened them again the room was full of sunlight and the door was sliding open. The only reason I could think of for the cell door opening was because it was breakfast time, but there was no way that much time had passed.

"Get that ass up," old man Doug said, pausing briefly at my door before continuing to get his tray.

My cellmate was still snoring, so I took the opportunity to get up and use the sink first. Two men in a cell was tight living, and the only way to co-exist was to take turns in order to avoid stepping on each other's toes. After brushing my teeth and washing my face, I decided to do the decent thing and wake him up so he wouldn't miss breakfast. I put on my green jumpsuit and my black jail-issued converse and stepped out to face another day of the same ol' bullshit.

"Took you long enough, youngin'. I was 'bout to eat your tray."

"Pops, you eat my tray and I'ma make sure you can't chew shit else for a while," I said, accepting the milk he handed me as we both got in line to be handed a tray.

Nothing good ever came on a jail tray, but the deputies were still the ones to hand them out to ensure everyone got their fair share of slop. This morning's fine cuisine consisted of grits, potatoes, two biscuits, and what passed for meaty gravy, which we all called shit on a shingle. As bad as it sounded, it was actually one of the best things they served.

"What's the plan for the day, pops?" I asked old man Doug, taking a seat next to him at one of the two metal tables in the pod.

"You know the routine: coffee, honeybuns, and some cards."

"Yeah, I could use something to take my mind off the ol' girl," I replied.

"Ol' girl? You talking about that ex you were telling me about, or the mystery lady with the pretty handwriting and scented letters?"

"I ain't letting Elyse keep me from getting sleep," I said, frontin' like my heart wasn't still hurt.

"So, it's the girl with the mean pen game, then."

"Yeah. I called my mom's last night and she tells me some female left a message with a phone number for me to call, but she didn't leave her name."

"And you think it's the same one who's been writing you?" he asked.

"Who else would it be? I been fuckin' with the same bitch for the last few years, and everybody knew that."

"Yeah, but maybe they know you ain't rockin' with her no more and they see this as the perfect time to get at you," he suggested with a wink.

"The perfect time? My man, I'm up against three homicides right now. If there was ever a wrong time, this is it!"

"What use is speculating? Put your big boy pants on and call whoever it is. You scared or naw?" he asked, smiling mischievously.

The fact he was missing his two front teeth made it hard to keep a straight face when he flashed that smile, and it made it even harder to back down. We both went about eating our breakfast, but every time I looked at him he gave me that same goofy-ass grin. We called him "old man" or "pops" mainly because of his teeth, because in all actuality he didn't look that old. He was probably two or three inches shorter than me with a bald head and a wiry mustache, but he didn't have that hard face you saw on a lot of older black men.

That face symbolized the struggle was real, but the old man was proof incarceration could preserve you better than Botox. One of the things I admired most about old man Doug was the fact he loved to laugh and have fun despite our environment. Right now his laughter was coming at my expense, and I could see it dancing in his whiskey-colored eyes. When I'd told him about Elyse he'd called me "tender dick" before telling me there was plenty more pussy where hers came from if I wasn't afraid to go get it.

"What have I got to lose?" I said, getting up and going to the phone.

I had a moment's hesitation when I was reaching in my sock for the number because calling someone's house this early in the morning could get a muthafucka cussed out. Then again, whoever she is might be at work, so the odds were good my call would go unanswered anyway. I dialed the number and tried to convince myself not to hang up when it finally started ringing. I didn't hear when she picked up, but I knew it had to either be her or her answering machine, because the automated message the jail provided was running its course.

"Hello?"

"H-Hi," I said attentively.

"Well, if it isn't the infamous Ahmani Monroe. I was wondering when you'd call," she said, laughing.

Her voice was sweet, melodic even, and undoubtedly belonging to a white girl.

"I almost didn't call. I mean, this is all kinda weird to me."

"I get that, and I didn't want it to be, so I guess I should explain myself. Let me start by saying I know you didn't do what you're accused of, and I feel bad you have to sit in jail while you prove your innocence. I was hoping my letters would take your mind off of things, if only for a little while."

"Well you succeeded in doing that, but I still don't understand why. I mean, we don't even know each other," I said.

"You're right, we don't, but I've seen you around before at parties in Iron Gate and Georgetown South. I even saw you at the apartments in Carlisle Station."

Her recounting of places we'd crossed paths had me even more curious than I already was because she was naming some rough neighborhoods, and couldn't no average white girl navigate through them.

"Are you gonna tell me your name?" I asked.

"Eventually, yeah, but right now ain't the time to do that."

"Okay, so tell me how this works. Am I just gonna keep getting anonymous mail describing your attraction for me?" I could hear her laughing softly before she responded.

"I can't lie, writing you letters has helped take my mind off of a lot of shit that's been going on in my life at the moment. I'm getting over a bad breakup, and I'm also dealing with recent tragedy."

"Sorry to hear that," I said sincerely.

"It's life, I guess, but knowing that still doesn't ease the pain or guilt. Anyway, you've been a welcome distraction. So much so that I wanna get to know you better."

"Oh yeah? I thought you knew me pretty well based on how certain you are I didn't kill three people," I said, hoping she would show her crazy if there was any to be seen.

"I don't have to know you to know you didn't kill that family, Ahmani, but I do wanna know everything about you before you get out."

"And why is that?" I asked.

"Because I don't give the pussy up to guys I don't know."

That statement was reassuring when compared to my ex's philosophy about spreading her legs, but the underlying implication had me at a loss for words. It would seem sex was a forgone conclusion for us, and that way of thinking might be the first indicator of her crazy.

"Okay," I replied slowly.

"Calm down. I ain't a ho, and I ain't cray-cray. We know some of the same people, so rest assured I'll come to you with references when the time's right. For now, let's just have fun."

"Fun? Sweetheart, I don't know if you've noticed, but I'm sitting in jail about to go on trial for my life. This shit ain't fun!" I replied, damn near certain this bitch had to be crazy.

"Yeah, but you're not guilty, and that'll be proven soon."

"I sincerely appreciate the vote of confidence, but you don't know what you're talking about. The odds of me walking away from this are —"

"Trust me," she said.

"Trust you? Slim, I don't even know you, so how do you expect me to trust you on this situation?"

"Because I know what I'm talking about. I know you didn't do it, Ahmani, but I know who did."

Chapter Three

I could taste the stale air moving across my tongue, alerting me to the fact my mouth was wide open. At first I thought I must've heard her wrong, because there was no way she'd just said she knew who'd really killed the people I was accused of killing. I could literally feel my heart knocking all the way up to my teeth, but I forced myself to take a much-needed deep breath before I spoke a word.

"Say that again."

"I know you heard me, and you heard me correctly too. I know you didn't kill anyone because I know who did it, but I don't know why."

"I'm not focused on the why right now, I just wanna know if you're full of shit. And if you ain't, then why the fuck am I still in here?" I asked.

"I'm not full of shit, and you'll be out of there soon. I promise."

My mind was blown listening to her talk. This bitch was nothing more than a voice on the phone and some freak shit in a letter, but here she was promising me my freedom. In what world was this reality?

"Listen, I'm sure you're a nice girl and all that, but I'm really not interested in broken promises. This shit is real life, so you have a nice day while I get back to living it."

"Talk to your lawyer," she said just before I hung up the phone.

From the moment I'd gotten that first letter I'd wondered, but now that I'd actually talked to her I knew she was coo-coo.

"Well?" old man Doug asked when I sat back down at the table.

"You don't even want the details, but trust me when I tell you she's loco for certain."

His immediate laughter didn't help the situation at all, but eventually I joined in because I knew I'd at least have one helluva story to tell.

We got up and pushed our trays back out the slot in the door to the deputies before getting to our usual daily activities. Old man Doug swore he was the tabletop champion, claiming to be the best at any card game, dominos, chess, checkers, and everything in between. He was nice, but I was a fast learner, and soon the student was gonna be the one handing out ass-whoopings to the teacher. Once we had ourselves set up with everything we'd need for a few hours, we got down to business.

We had two games of pinnacle and three games of spades under our belts before the deputy came back through with lunch sacks. Every day lunch was either two bologna sandwiches or two salami sandwiches and some type of fruit that had seen better days. The only way to survive this jail was with commissary, but I was low on snacks, so I couldn't miss many meals.

"You want this orange?" I offered.

"If you know like I do, you'll eat that and get all the Vitamin C you can. It's easy to get sick in here and hard to get rid of it."

I knew he was telling the truth because a muthafucka was always sniffling. The fact the air conditioning was kept at blizzard levels didn't help, but they said it reduced germs. My best bet was to do what the old man said and eat my orange.

"Man, I can't wait for them to pass commissary," I said.

"Me too, but I'm more interested in seeing that pretty young thing who brings the food around. I'd eat her and say damn the honeybuns!"

"You an old freak," I said, laughing with him.

"I'll be that, but that's better than a lot of these niggas who fuck ass and suck —"

Our conversation was interrupted by the sound of the intercom clicking on overhead. Whenever the intercom came on, everybody shut up because it meant someone was about to be called out of the pod for some reason.

"Monroe!"

"Yeah?" I replied, looking at old man Doug, confused.

"Attorney visit."

I knew damn well my usual lazy-ass public pretender wasn't there to see me, which only left one option.

"Yo, this lawyer must be official, because I just got the court paper last night saying he'd been assigned to my case."

"What's his name?" old man Doug asked.

"Michael Sprano."

"Oh yeah, I've heard of him. He's a good dude, and he knows his shit."

"I hope you're right," I said, getting up and going to the door where the deputy stood waiting.

Most inmates were allowed to go to attorney visits, programs, or to see the chaplain without an escort, but my max security status meant I had to have a cop with me anywhere I went outside of my pod. I'd never required this type of supervision in my previous jail visits, so it was kinda weird to me, but even weirder were the looks of both fear and respect I got from other inmates in the hallways. From what I understood about the system, killers were revered, which was completely opposite of how society saw them.

We weren't in the streets no more, though. This was the entrance to the jungle, and very few made it out alive. I was determined to defy the odds, though, because I didn't belong here. Not for murder, anyway.

During my walk through the halls and the ride down in the elevator, my mind kept going back to my conversation with the crazy chick this morning. Was it just a coincidence my lawyer had showed up today, or did this woman somehow know what she was talking about? I wanted to hope, but that could be a dangerous thing, because on the other side of hope was devastation.

When we came to the attorney visitation rooms, I took a much-needed breath before walking in. There were several rooms to choose from, some on the right and others on the left, but all completely see-through and monitored by video cameras to prevent the passing of contraband. I had no idea what my new lawyer looked like, so I walked slowly up the aisle between rooms until I was flagged down. Entering the room, I sized him up, taking in his five-foot, eight-inch frame and the obviously tailored blue pinstriped suit with the baby blue shirt and red tie. I noticed the Movado, the manicure, and the haircut just as quickly as I did the blue gators.

This white boy had taste, but my rapid assessment led to the comforting conclusion he had money. In his profession, money only came from being damn good at what you do, and it looked like he was upper echelon, especially if the diamonds in the face of his watch were real.

"Have a seat, Mr. Monroe, I'm your new lawyer, Michael Sprano," he said, offering his hand to shake.

I shook it before sitting across the cheap wooden table from him. The room we were in was definitely no bigger than my cell, and most of the space was taken up by the table between us. But even if it hadn't been, I had the feeling this slight-build man could give the illusion of filling up any room.

"You got here quick. I only got the letter telling me you were on my case last night."

"I work fast, and I get results. But truthfully, I've been working on your case for almost a week now."

"Really? Well, I need to tell you from the jump I didn't kill nobody, and I don't—"

"I know that," he said smoothly.

"You-you know that? Now, when you say that, do you mean you believe in all your clients' innocence?"

"Of course not. I've been around a long time, and I know more often than not my clients are guilty, but yours is a different situation.

"How so?" I asked, feeling hope wanting to take ahold of me again.

"Well, you did break into the Hudsons' home and steal more than $5,000 in cash and jewelry. That part you're guilty of. It was simply your misfortune two people were killed and their daughter went missing."

"They're charging me with her murder, too, even though they don't have a body. That's bullshit!" I said, frustrated.

"Don't worry, all the murder charges will be dropped, so we just need to worry about—"

"Hold up, what do you mean all the murder charges will be dropped? How? When?"

"I get the feeling there's a lot you don't know, so maybe I should start from the beginning. Of course, you know everything we discuss is covered by attorney-client privilege, right?"

"Yeah," I replied, somewhat impatiently.

"It's true I'm one of the top defense attorneys in Northern Virginia, and the courts did assign your case to me, but I knew about you even before that. A few days after the murders made front page and television news, I was contacted by a young woman who told me the suspect the cops arrested was innocent. Naturally, I thought she was a friend of yours, maybe a family member, or just some chick you were fucking. I mean, you were pulled over not far from the scene damn near right after the shit happened, and you still had the stolen shit on you. Nobody in the world would've thought you weren't all kinds of guilty! However, one thing that was interesting was the fact Katrina Hudson wasn't found with you or at the scene, which meant you either had an accomplice or there was something else going on."

"I don't work with anyone. That way I don't have to worry about somebody cutting a deal against me, and I have no idea where the girl is," I said defiantly.

"I know all of that. I've reviewed your record and I know you work alone. As for Katrina Hudson, no one knows where she is, but I promise you she's alive and well. I can see the confused look on your face, but if you'll bear with me, all will be explained. Okay, so I asked the caller how she knows you're not guilty, and she explained how the couple was already dead when you got there, but because they were stabbed to death while they slept, you probably mistook them for sleeping."

"I did," I said, shaking my head at how wrong I'd been. There I was creeping around their bedroom thinking I was being slick when I was really robbing some dead folks. There had to be a special place in hell for that type of shit!

"Well, apparently you and the killer missed each other by minutes, which works out in your favor because you probably would've got bodied too. Katrina managed to get away despite a few bumps, bruises, and cuts, which explains the blood trail the cops found."

"So, if she got away, where the fuck is she? And why have I not been cleared yet?" I asked, feeling the hope I'd been fighting come to life in full force inside me.

"From what I understand, Katrina is hiding because the killer is someone she considered a friend, and she doesn't know why he'd want her and her family dead. She's worried he still might be after her."

"Not to sound harsh, but that ain't my problem! I'm about to get buried for some shit I didn't do, and I don't got time to be worried about why these rich white people got toe-tagged," I said truthfully.

"Well then, I guess it's a good thing the surviving rich white girl don't want you to go down for something you didn't do."

"What do you mean?"

"What I mean is the girl who called me was actually Katrina herself. She's hesitant to come out in public for the reasons I mentioned, but she's never wanted to see you go down for some shit you didn't do. She wanted to tell you all this herself, but due to her wanting to fly under the radar, she thought sending you letters of encouragement would keep your spirits up."

Instantly everything made sense in a way it hadn't before. Not only had I gotten letters from the girl I was accused of killing, but I'd fucking talked to her a few hours ago!

"That's who been writing me? You're bullshittin', right?"

"I assure you I'm not, Ahmani, but now you understand why there was never a return address or name on anything. She's been working behind the scenes with me to prove you didn't do this, and to find out why it happened in the first place. I was told to show you this," he said, taking a picture from his pocket and placing it on the table in front of me.

I'd seen pictures of Katrina before on the news of course, and there had always been a faint familiarity, but the picture he slid my way brought it all home. In this photo her jet-black hair was piled high on top of her head in a messy bun, and her blue eyes were slightly out of focus. The black knee-length leather skirt and matching halter top she wore only succeeded in enhancing her thickness and curves, and seeing her like this made me wonder how I'd ever forgotten her. The picture was from graduation night, or rather the after party in Cover Stone Apartments that had turned into a block party. I was gung-ho that night, but I remembered seeing her and wondering what this thick-ass white girl was doing slumming with us in the projects.

"I've seen her before," I said.

"Katrina figured you'd remember her better from this night in particular, especially since you defended her honor."

I thought that statement was putting a lot on it. I mean, all I'd done was put the beats to a nigga who'd decided to get rough with her because she didn't wanna leave with him. Sometimes girls gave guys mixed signals when they were playing hard-to-get with the pussy, but Katrina had been stating loud and clear she had no intentions on fucking him or anyone else. A bruised ego had led to a devastating ass whooping for the ol' boy, but it had the potential to lead me to freedom now.

"So, what's next?" I asked.

"Katrina has already provided me with an affidavit absolving you for the murders, but before I go to the cops with that, I wanna negotiate a deal on the burglary and larceny charges. I'm sure we'll get a sweet deal despite your priors because the prosecution thinks the murders are a slam dunk."

"What if they ask to see Katrina? I mean, they're gonna want to know who committed the crimes, and your word or some piece of paper ain't gonna be good enough."

"The name is included in the affidavit, along with an accurate accounting of what went down at her house that night. As for her appearing in the flesh, she's agreed to do that one time when I actually give the paperwork to the police, and then she's going back into hiding."

"When?" I asked, finally feeling freedom within my grasp.

"I'm going to the D.A. after I leave here to get your deal done, and then it just depends on how long it takes

Katrina to get back to Manassas. Hopefully you'll be out within the next 48 hours."

Chapter Four

Hey, handsome! By the time, you get this, you should have gotten a visit from our mutual friend. I'm sorry I couldn't tell you exactly what was going on, but I'm sure you can understand my reasons now, and hopefully you don't think I'm a bad person. It's crazy to me how life has thrown us together again after all the time that's passed, but I believe everything happens for a reason. I'm still searching for a reason to a lot of mysteries. I want you to know I'm sorry you ended up in that situation, despite your initial reason for being in the wrong place at the wrong time. We may not come from the same household, but I've seen how real the struggle is. Hopefully when you're out of there you'll use your second chance wisely, because we both know the road you're on leads to nowhere. I'm not judging you, so please don't take it that way. I just think you're better than what you do. And if you're really pressed for money, you should take up boxing. LOL! I can't tell you how many times I've replayed that night in my mind, but not just because of the punishment you handed out. To be real with you, that shit turned me on, and you probably didn't know it, but you definitely could've got what that dude wanted. Who knows, maybe you'll still get it one of these days. If you can handle it. See you soon....

I must've read her letter five times since they'd done mail call, not only for the sexual innuendo, but because it actually meant everything me and my lawyer talked about was real. I'd wanted to tell old man Doug the good news, but part of me felt like if I spoke on it out loud I'd jinx the whole thing. I was determined to bite my tongue off before I did that, but my mind never strayed far from thinking about everything that was about to go down. It was hard to imagine being free in a matter of days after facing the threat of life in prison. It felt like I was dreaming, and if that was the case, I was gonna be pissed when I woke up!

Even though I hadn't confided in old man Doug about what was exactly said, I knew he knew it was serious because I'd done nothing except pace around the pod since I came back in. I'd wanted to proceed with my day and kill time as usual, but I couldn't make myself sit still. I doubted I'd get any sleep!

I wanted to call my mom and tell her the good news if for no other reason than to put her mind at ease, but Mr. Sprano said I had to play it cool until all the papers were signed. I had no idea what type of sweet deal he was shooting for, but I wasn't looking down the barrel at six hundred years, and that was a blessing. Katrina had literally given me a second chance at life, and that thought alone had been tickling the corners of my mind all day. Anybody would've thought she was crazy if all they had to go on were the letters she sent me and the conversation we'd had earlier. But she wasn't crazy; she was scared and cautious, and I'd hung up on her.

I felt the need to apologize, but I wasn't sure how to go about it. Pride was a muthafucka, and it had no business in this situation because I was dead-ass wrong. Taking a deep breath, I refolded her latest letter and put it back in its envelope before heading toward the phone. I didn't need to pull her number out of my sock since I'd spent enough time looking at it and memorizing it. The battle within on whether or not I should make this call had started the moment I found out who she was, but now that the time had come I felt no nervousness. Before I knew it the phone was ringing, and after four rings I was about to hang up when I suddenly heard her voice.

"Hey."

"Hey yourself," she replied, slightly out of breath.

"Did I catch you at a bad time?"

"No, I was just getting out of the shower and my phone was in the other room. I was expecting your call."

"Were you?" I asked.

"Well, expecting is probably the wrong word. I should say I was hoping you'd call."

"And why is that?"

"Because I know how crazy I must've sounded to you, and I hated not being able to keep shit all the way real. So I was hoping when you finally heard the truth you'd reconsider us getting to know each other," she replied.

"I got your letter today."

"Did you?"

"Yeah, and I remember the night that picture was taken," I said.

"I thought you might, although I was wondering what part you'd remember more vividly: the situation or what I was wearing?"

Her question caught me off guard and made me laugh. The other funny thing was I didn't remember her voice sounding this sexy in our last conversation.

"Your outfit was memorable, but I'm wondering if you look the same. You know, it's been two years since I've last seen you."

"My hair is a little shorter, my eyes a little bluer, but I'm still five foot with the body of a thoroughbred," she replied confidently.

"Hmm. I'm not sure how to respond to that."

"I want you to say whatever comes to mind."

"That's easy. Damn!" I replied, laughing.

Her laughter was soft and it carried an effortless seduction with it. It was kinda like listening to some old-school R&B.

"Is that all you wanna say?" she asked.

"What do you want me to say?"

"I want you to be real with me. I mean, now you know who's behind all the letters, and you know who I am and what I look like. I want you to tell me what you'd do to me."

When I opened my mouth to speak, I had to close it again and swallow. This chick ain't believe in beatin' around the bush! For some niggas that might be intimidating, but just because I was locked up didn't mean I lost my swag.

"What I'd do to you, huh? To be honest, I'd probably taste you first, because I don't believe in putting my dick anywhere my tongue won't go."

"Hmm, really?" she purred.

"True shit. After that I might have you ride this dick reverse cowgirl-style so I can watch your ass jiggle."

"I've got a lot of ass, too."

"I remember. Depending on how freaky you are, I might have to get in that ass, too."

"Does that mean you'll put your tongue there, too?" she said seductively.

"Only when you're mine would you get that special treatment."

"I-I'm already yours, bae," she replied, breathing more heavily with each passing second.

"What are you doing?"

"I-I'm listening to you and p-playing with my pussy."

"Are you gonna cum just from the sound of my voice?" I asked softly.

"Mm-hm, if-if you let me."

"If I let you? So, you're saying that pussy belongs to me, then?"

"Y-yes, daddy!" she panted.

I could hear the need in her voice, and even though it was strictly against jail etiquette, I turned away from everyone to hide my arousal. I'd always tried to get Elyse to have phone sex with me during my short stints in jail, but she always had some excuse for why it wasn't gonna happen. It was evident Katrina was 'bout that action, and that was a huge turn-on.

"You like it rough?"

"Yes, daddy!"

"So, when I grab you by your hair, bend you over, and tell you to take this dick, you gonna take it?"

"Y-yes daddy! C-can I cum now?"

"No. I want you to stop what you're doing," I told her. I could still hear her breathing heavily, but I didn't hear her moving anymore.

"How wet are you?"

"I'm soaking wet."

"Put the phone in between your legs and let me hear you play with your pussy," I demanded.

There were some brief rustling noises, and then a sound no one could ever confuse with anything other than pussy talking to them. I'd never heard anything so sweet or a female who got that wet without physically having a nigga inside them. She had my shit throbbing so hard it was painful!

"Did you hear it?"

"I did. Now cum for me," I said, wishing I could concentrate hard enough to teleport myself to where she was.

Her moans intensified, and within thirty seconds she was screaming my name like it was the key to religious freedom. In that moment I didn't know who was more open, me or her. One thing I did know was I was damn sure gonna need a cold shower before I even thought about sleep tonight.

"I needed that," she said, laughing softly.

"I see, but now you got me over here all the way sexually frustrated."

"Aw, I'm sorry! I promise I'll make it up to you real soon."

"Oh yeah? How?" I asked.

"Ahmani I wasn't just saying shit in the moment. I want you to come home and tattoo your name in this pussy. I mean, if you're up to it."

"If I'm up to it? Consider that challenge accepted, but what I want to know is when exactly will I be coming home?" I replied seriously.

"As soon as I get that call from the lawyer, I'm gonna do my part, I promise. Believe me, I want you out of there."

"Just for the sex, huh?"

"Oh, I want way more than that from you, Ahmani Monroe."

"How do you know that? You don't even know me," I said.

"I'll tell you what I know. I know where you come from, but despite that you're still a good guy who knows right from wrong. Would you break the law? Sure, but who doesn't in some way, whether it's large or small? I know you're not a dummy, and this is evidenced by your lack of co-defendants, because you know most muthafuckas can't hold water. I feel like I know the character of the man you are, and what I don't know now, I'm hoping you'll show me when you get out."

It was sounding like she wanted more than to just get her feathers plucked, but honestly I didn't know if I was in any condition to give her that. My relationship with Elyse had taken a lot out of me, but I'd be lying if I said Katrina didn't have my attention. Loyalty was a big deal, and she seemed like she had that to give.

"I'ma keep it one hundred with you, I'm still emotionally fucked up from my last breakup, so I'm not sure if I can be everything you want me to be," I said.

"I don't want you to be anything other than yourself. I'm not saying we should get married your first day home, because like I mentioned before, I too am dealing with a rough breakup. But I do wanna kick it with you, and I ain't no ho, so even when I am just talking to a dude, I'm exclusive."

I didn't respond right away because I didn't want her to know how much I was feeling what she was kickin' at me. It all sounded good, but only time could tell how real she was.

"I'm down to see what happens when I'm a free man, if you plan on sticking around."

"For you, I will," she replied in that same seductive voice that made the hair on the back of my neck salute.

I was ready to say something smart when the automated voice came over the line announcing we had one minute left before our call would end.

"Can you call me back, bae?" she asked.

"There's a line for the phone, and I'd hate to catch an assault charge when freedom is right around the corner. I'll try to get back in line, though."

"Please do. I enjoyed talking to you, even though your voice makes me horny as shit," she replied, laughing.

"If that makes you horny, wait until you see my —"

Our conversation was cut off just before I could describe what I was planning to slay her with. Reluctantly I hung up and told the dude behind me to let me get back when he was finished. I knew somebody was gonna be upset about me being on their lawn and using the phone again, but they'd just have to get over that.

"What's up with you?" old man Doug asked, walking up on me.

"What you mean?"

"You been in another world since that lawyer came to see you, and then I came out of my cell to find you huddled up on the phone with your back to the whole pod. What's going on, young nigga?'

"Ah, it ain't shit, for real. I was just kickin' it with ol' girl," I replied nonchalantly.

"Oh, I know who you were talking to, nigga. I can see all your teeth!"

I'd been trying to keep a straight face, but now I had to laugh out loud. "Ayo, slim is crazy," I said, shaking my head as I thought about what had happened during our phone call.

"Yeah, you told me that earlier."

"Nah, I mean she's crazy in a good way. This morning I said she was crazy because she came at me talking 'bout she knew I didn't kill nobody because she knew who really did it."

"Oh yeah. And she does?" he asked, looking at me closer.

I hadn't meant to open my mouth and put both of my damn feet in it, but that's exactly what I'd done. Old man Doug had been shooting straight with me from the jump, and truthfully there was nothing to fear because I was going home. Why not tell him?

"Let's go to your cell really quick," I said, looking around to see who was watching us as we disappeared.

"A'ight, look, what I'm about to tell you is gonna sound crazy, and trust me, I'm still trying to wrap my mind around everything that's happened."

"Spit it out, my nigga. I been around a long time, so I done heard it all," he replied confidently.

"You think you heard it all, old man, but you haven't. Let's start with the fact the mystery woman is someone I'm accused of killing."

Aryanna

Chapter Five

The agony of slow time was only comparable to the regret of wasted time. It had been two whole days since my initial conversation with my lawyer, and a day since I signed the plea deal he'd brokered. The fact the prosecutor actually agreed to time served and probation on two felonies showed they really felt they had me cold on the bodies. Damn, I wanted to be a fly on that wall when their case fell apart before their eyes! I'd settle for just being let the fuck out of jail, though. Being in this situation got old quick, and this experience actually had me reconsidering my means of making money.

True enough, my conversations with Katrina had led to me questioning the wisdom in continuing my profession, but really, I was tired of getting locked up. I wasn't even old enough to buy liquor, but I was old enough for the system to throw a life sentence at me. That in itself was a scary thought — a sobering one, though. Ever since I'd called Katrina back after our initial misunderstanding, we'd spent almost every free moment on the phone talking about what the future might look like. It wasn't as if we were planning our wedding, but the truth was the same event had forever changed the both of us, and that kinda bonded us.

Individually we had to find a way to move on and a direction to take, but the chemistry between us was undeniable. I didn't know when I'd ever laughed so much with a woman. Admittedly, at first I was just thinking we had a sexual connection because she loved to play with herself with me on the phone, and that was hot! But we talked, too, and I actually found myself waiting to hear what she had to say. There was never an awkward silence or the feeling of strained conversation; we just flowed. Old man Doug teased me about falling in love the first time I smelled the pussy, but I laughed that off for the nonsense it was. I couldn't lie, though, I was hella curious about Katrina's head game, because she bragged on that shit like it was the holy grail.

Some dudes would've been put off by that, because all they would be able to imagine is all the dicks she'd sucked to get good at it. I wasn't a hypocrite, though. I'd eaten my fair share of pussy as a young nigga, because I wanted to be good enough to make a bitch see Jesus. If her skill set matched mine, then we were definitely in for some fireworks whenever I got the fuck out of here!

"What's good, young nigga? You up for a game of dominoes?" old man Doug asked, sitting across from me at the table.

"It's 7:00 p.m. on Thursday night, and I ain't got no date, so I guess I can bust your ass real quick."

"Now, you know you ain't got a win coming, but at least you don't lack confidence," he replied, grabbing the dominoes from the middle of the table and dumping them in between us. "I'm surprised you ain't on the phone."

"I'll probably call her later on. I was hoping I'd be out today so I could actually see her, or at least Facetime with her," I said, trying to hide my disappointment.

"Shit like this takes time. This system is rigged, and it ain't in our favor, so when the rare occasion comes around where we're actually innocent, it burns their ass to turn us loose. It'll happen, though, because they don't have a choice."

I knew he was right, but being patient about my freedom wasn't easy. I had shit to do! When I'd thought spending the rest of my life in prison was a forgone conclusion, I started thinking about all the shit I'd never do. I wanted to go places outside of the hood. I wanted kids and a wife. I wanted to be something other than a statistic like so many of my niggas who were either in the ground or doing numbers in some facility.

"I feel you, pops. I guess I better learn some type of patience if I'ma make it out there, huh?"

"You damn straight. I ain't one to lecture you on never coming back, though, because I've made this my home away from home. You gotta decide what you want out of life," he replied seriously.

"I'm working on it. I —"

"Monroe!" the deputy yelled from the door.

"Here," I called out, turning around to go get my mail.

He didn't have any mail in his hands, though, just a piece of paper and a trash bag.

"I'm Monroe," I said once I got to the door.

"B&B," he replied, handing me the trash bag.

Those were the two sweetest initials any man wanted to hear in this situation, because they stood for bed and baggage. I was going home. I took the bag from his hand in a daze, feeling like this moment was surreal despite how much I'd been anticipating it. My mind had believed I'd be let out, but my heart hadn't accepted it until this very moment. The looks I got as I made my way to my cell were both those of envy and hate, but I couldn't blame them because every man in here was looking at doing a bid. I motioned for old man Doug to come with me while I tried to quiet the screaming in my head long enough to figure out what my first move would be.

"I told you, young nigga. And you're lucky, too, because I was just about to hurt your feelings on that domino table."

Doug was smiling, but I could see in his eyes he was gonna miss me. Bonds were formed sometimes in this environment, not just because we were living this hell together, but because there were voids that needed filling. I never knew my father and I didn't let that affect me or how I lived. It was nice to have an older man take me under his wing and teach me what I didn't know in order to survive, because it was something I didn't have. I know old man Doug had kids out there he didn't get to see because of his constant run-ins with the law, and I knew he missed them, so our bond had formed out of a necessity for both of us that neither of us could articulate because that's not how shit was done. We had an understanding, though, and I was gonna miss him as much as he would me.

"You were right, pops. And I don't know whose ass you was 'bout to kick at dominos, but it wasn't mine. We need to have a serious convo real quick," I said, going to my tote where my mail, hygiene, and commissary were kept.

"Ain't no time to talk, fool. You gotta get out of here and —"

"Just listen, old man. I know niggas make promises every day 'bout what they gonna do for a nigga on the outside, and then they get amnesia once they wash the funk of the jail off them. The only promise I'ma make you is I'm never gonna change the type of dude I am, meaning I'ma fuck with you the long way for life. I don't know exactly where I'm gonna be, but I want you to use this number by noon tomorrow, and I'll know more then."

I quickly scribbled down my cell phone number and passed it to him before gathering the little mail I had and tossing it in my bag.

"Ahmani, you know you don't owe me nothing."

"That's right, I don't owe you nothing, especially not no lies. Use the number, my nigga," I said, looking him squarely in the eye and hoping all I couldn't say would reveal itself.

In a move seldom seen in this environment, he pulled me in for a quick hug that made me smile.

"A'ight, you ol' sappy muthafucka, it's time for me to shake this spot."

"Hold up, you leaving all your food and shit," he said.

Behind these walls commissary was currency, and I'd just got a hundred dollars' worth of zoom zooms and wham whams yesterday, which was a big deal in here. It wouldn't mean shit to me on the street, though.

"Man, quit bullshittin', and get that shit to your house before you get mugged," I said, giving him a wink as I walked out of the cell and to the front door.

There were no well wishes, only mean mugs and whispers under the breath that no doubt were implying I'd snitched on someone to get out. I wasn't mad, though, because I understand everything is based on perception and what people think they knew. Shit, I probably would've been thinking the same thing if a muthafucka with a high-profile case like mine was suddenly going free. Their opinions didn't matter, though. As I walked out the door and down the hallways to booking where I'd change out, my thoughts were on how I'd capitalized on my second chance.

Opportunities like this didn't come along often, so to not fully seize them was like spitting in God's face.

Once I got into the changing room, I quickly stripped out of the jumpsuit and cheap shoes, pulling on my navy blue Black Billionaire sweatpants, t-shirt, hoodie, and stepping into my baby blue and navy Air Force Ones. It was amazing how just having on my own clothes made me feel so much more human than I had five minutes ago. I came out of the changing room and went to the front desk next to the metal door that was the barrier between me and fresh air.

"Sign here for your property, Mr. Monroe," a male deputy said, pushing me a piece of paper and a large manila envelope.

Opening it, I found my cell phone and my gold chain with a cross attached to it my mom had given me for my eighteenth birthday. I'd had some cash when I came in, but the cops had confiscated it, saying I had no job to verify income, which probably meant I'd stolen all of it from the Hudson family. I put my chain on, put my phone in my pocket, tossed the envelope in the trash, and scribbled my name on the paper. Once the deputy saw my signature, he signaled whatever officer was in the tinted-out control booth and the door beside me slid open with a loud whoosh of air.

"You're free to go."

I damn near wanted to cry at hearing those words, but not another moment or tear would be wasted in this place. With my mail in hand, I quickly made my way out front, taking in big gulps of the fresh night air and admiring the stars for their beauty that often went unnoticed.

"Nice night, isn't it?"

Her voice startled me, but she was definitely a sight for sore eyes. I hadn't expected to see her this soon, but she damn sure wasn't a disappointment in her tight stonewashed jeans, black thigh-high boots, and black cashmere sweater that hung off her shoulder, revealing one of her black bra straps. Her hair hung just above her shoulders, and even with the ten-foot distance between us I could see the sparkle in her blue eyes and the shine of her lip-gloss.

"Thought you were supposed to be in hiding," I said, walking toward her.

"Oh, I am. I've been in the police station all day giving my statement and waiting on them to release you. In fact, there are probably cops watching me right now, but they're definitely watching the man responsible for killing my parents."

"I'm sorry for your loss," I said sincerely.

For a brief moment she looked away from me, and I could tell she was gathering her composure. It took strength beyond measure to survive what she was going through. I mean, I couldn't even imagine how I'd be if something happened to my mom.

"Nice ride," I said, changing the subject in hopes of avoiding the obvious pain she was is.

"Thanks. It was a gift."

"A 2015 Jeep Wrangler unlimited ain't no gift, it's a statement," I replied, stopping a few feet away from her and the truck she was leaning against.

She had it laid out in flat black with matching thirty-inch rims on it, and it was tinted to the legal limit.

"Boys and cars. Guess it's a good thing I didn't drive my dad's Maybach Coupe," she said, shaking her head.

"You own a Maybach Coupe?"

"And a few other toys. But before we discuss my net worth, can I get a hug?" she asked, opening her arms and stepping toward me.

I complied without hesitation, pulling her into my arms while inhaling the sweet scent of jasmine coming from her skin. The moment our bodies touched, every erotic conversation we had and letter she'd written me flashed in my mind, and I knew I couldn't hold onto her for too long.

"I know I stink, smelling like jail and shit," I said, taking a step back.

"Actually, you don't," she replied, looking up at me with those big blue eyes that twinkled in the darkness with more than a hint of mischief.

"You're just being nice, but a nigga needs a shower."

"Well, by all means, let's go," she said, handing me the keys and opening the passenger door.

"You want me to drive?"

"You're gonna have to, because I don't know where we're going," she replied, climbing into the truck.

I went around to the driver's side and got in, but I didn't start the engine.

"There's some important things we need to discuss before we just ride off into the sunset," I said, looking over at her.

"You have a lot of questions, and I get that, so let's start with the obvious. My parents were killed by a guy named Aaron Charles. We used to date, and when I broke up with him he went crazy, but I never thought he'd try to kill me and my family. That night he'd called a couple of times saying we needed to talk, but I ignored him. A noise woke me up, and when I went to see what it was, he was coming out of my parent's room holding a bloody knife. He came for me, and I fought him with everything I had until I finally was able to hit him in the nuts and run away. I was terrified. I mean, I couldn't understand why he would kill my parents when they were actually fond of him, once upon a time. Aaron comes from money, so I knew he'd use whatever influences he had to get to me, which meant I had to get gone and stay gone. There was no way for me to know you'd get caught up in this mess, and when I saw you'd been arrested, I thought the cops would figure out their fuck-up."

"It looked too good from their prospective, so once they had me in custody, that was the end of their search for suspects. Hell, they'd even stopped looking for you and were simply content to charge my black ass with another count of murder!" I said, still disgusted with how I was handled.

"I couldn't watch you go out like that, but I needed time to figure out what to do and how to do it. I hope you're not mad at me for taking so long," she said, taking my hand in hers with a pleading look in her eyes.

"Katrina, I don't blame you in the slightest. I'm just glad you came forward at all, because it was not looking good for me."

"I hope you like how good it looks for you now," she said, smiling in a way that made my heart beat faster.

"Indeed, I do. You're gorgeous."

"Thank you. You don't look bad yourself, for a man that's been inside."

"Oh, don't worry, I clean up nicer than this with a hot shower and a fresh haircut with a lineup," I told her.

"Well, since I plan to be the only woman looking at you for a while, I say we can wait until tomorrow for the haircut. But a hot shower sounds promising."

"Do we know each other well enough to shower together? Because you know where that's gonna lead," I warned.

Her response was to take ahold of the front of my hoodie and pull me toward her. The softness of her lips made me shiver as she opened her mouth to me for exploration. I could taste the watermelon on her tongue as it introduced itself to mine eagerly, with both passion and obvious skill. My hands went to both sides of her face, allowing me to pull her deeper into my orbit and convey to her how she made me feel. I'd never had a first kiss that was so electrifying, and she had me wanting more.

"W-we gotta stop before we catch indecent charges," she said, reluctantly pulling away.

"Won't be nothing indecent about it," I said with a smile before kissing her quickly again and releasing my hold on her.

"Get us out of here. We've got places to go and things to do."

"I gotta make a stop first," I said.

"Wherever you go, I go. It's me and you."

Chapter Six

The look of surprised joy on my mom's face was one I'd never forget, but neither was the look of utter confusion that morphed into disapproval once she found out who Katrina was. My mother wasn't racially challenged, so it didn't matter I'd shown up on her doorstep with a white girl, but I could tell she was leery about this white girl. There was no open hostility or dirty looks, but I knew my mother, and I knew the way she had a hole in her tongue from biting it. We both sat down with her and explained the situation as best as we could while she listened to what Katrina had to say without going left on her. I felt the temperature change, though, when Katrina took my hand in hers while we sat on the couch.

Katrina was only a year younger than me, which meant we were both consenting adults and free to do whatever we felt like doing. It had been many years since my mother could or had told me what to do, and thankfully she was smart enough not to try to resurrect old habits now. So, we all played nice and sat around the living room, kicking the shit for a few hours. I wanted to wake my brother and sister up, but my mom had begged me not to because they'd had one of their rare bad days. When I agreed to let them sleep and just come back to visit them tomorrow, shit got interesting, because my mom suggested I spend the night. If part of my plea agreement had been to recount the last time I was invited into my mom's house for more than a few hours, my black ass would still be sitting in jail.

This wasn't the norm, and I could tell by the sudden increase in pressure Katrina was applying to my hand it wasn't what she'd had in mind. How could I say no? I mean, the more I thought about it, the more I could understand how the thought of losing me to the system forever had change my mom, too. After all, I was her first born.

Maybe my experience would bring us closer, and for that reason I agreed to stay, but in the same breath I let it be known Katrina and I were going to get something to eat real quick. For me not to spend a little time with her would've been ungrateful and insensitive.

From the moment we got back into her Jeep, I could tell she was feeling some type of way, but I wasn't sure how to begin wading through the minefield of a woman's emotions. Which was the reason we were sitting around the corner from my mom's house, eating our meals from Burger King in silence. Every time I looked at her, I got caught up in how beautiful she was. But I could feel the heat, and it wasn't coming from the whopper she was eating.

"I never met a girl who would eat in front of me," I commented.

"Yeah, well, these curves ain't get here by accident. Besides, ain't no need to fake like I don't eat, shit, or bleed once a month. I'm a woman."

"Oh, I have no doubts you're a woman. A pissed off woman, but a woman nonetheless."

When she cut her eyes in my direction, I thought she was getting ready to come at me sideways, but eventually I saw a small smile tugging at her lips.

"Your lips are amazing, you know?"

"Yeah, I know," she replied, wrapping them around her straw and sucking up some of her chocolate milkshake.

"You're a good kisser, too."

"You say that without any accusation or insecurity."

"Why would I come at you with either?" I asked.

"Come on, you know how you guys think. If a bitch kisses good and/or can suck the skin off the dick, it means she's had experience."

"And?"

"Most dudes are intimidated by that."

"I ain't most dudes, or didn't you already know that?" I asked, smiling.

"That's what your mouth says, but once you find out how good I am, you'll wonder."

"No, I won't. I'll just appreciate it, and I expect you to do the same when it comes to my skills."

For a moment she just stared at me, and I could see the challenge in her eyes. She took a slow sip of her shake while her hand shot out and was in my pants before I could utter a word. My dick had already been getting hard from watching her play with that straw in her mouth, but the moment she grabbed it, it stood up like Japanese steel!

"What are you —"

That's as far as I got before she pulled me free of my sweatpants and leaned over, taking damn near the whole thing in her mouth at once. The combination of fire and ice created a sensation what almost caused my spine to snap as I arched suddenly. The heat of her lips and mouth in competition with the remains of milkshake on her tongue had me wanting to scream for joy and beg for mercy all at once. As soon as I opened my mouth to do either, she took it to another level by pulling back slowly and concentrating on sucking the head while relaxing her throat muscles. And then she dove.

I knew from seeing females gag that taking all I had to offer wasn't an easy task, but I could feel Katrina's lips hit the base of my shaft as I made the back of her throat my new home. Some bitches lie about their head game, but my lack of breathing told me what real was, and her lack of mercy had the warning bells roaring in my head.

"K-K-Katrina, I —"

I couldn't even get the words out of my mouth because she was sucking harder now, pulling back until she only had the tip in her mouth before devouring me again. My hand went to her hair, but she grabbed it with surprising strength and pushed it away, determined to teach me who was in control. I lost track of the minutes, but sooner than my pride would've liked, I lost the fight with life and was introduced to a beautiful death. She caught every drop of my proteins in her mouth, even squeezing my shaft to make sure nothing escaped her.

And then, as if nothing happened, she sat back in her seat, picked the rest of her burger up from her lap, and went right back to eating.

I had so much I wanted to say, but breathing was still an obstacle. It took me a full ten minutes to get myself under control, and when I looked over at her she was eating french fries, staring blindly out the window into the night.

"Wow!" I finally managed to say.

"Bet you're wondering about my experience now, huh?"

"Baby, your past is of no interest to me. I was so fucked up by what just happened I'm praying it wasn't a one-time event!" I reply honestly.

When she looked at me, I could tell it was to search for deception, and for a split second I saw an insecure girl I hadn't known existed in this confident woman. As quick as you could blink, she was gone, and there was only mischief dancing in those blue eyes again.

"Whether or not it was a one-time thing depends on how good you eat pussy. To get head, you gotta give head."

"Oh, I have no problem with that. Believe me when I tell you I owe you for what you just did to me," I said.

"I'll give you a pass on how fast you came because you've been denied a woman's touch for a while, but I will warn you my pussy is just as good as my head, so you might want to prepare yourself."

I tried to laugh her comment off, but the look on her face was dead serious. Taking the remainder of her fries from her hand, I dropped them into the bag of trash between her feet, and then I reached for the buttons on her jeans.

I thought she might grab my hand to stop me, but she just continued to look steadily into my eyes, almost like she was daring me. With her pants unbuttoned and unzipped, I'd expected the feel the lace of some sexy panties, but instead I came into contact with her smooth skin. Hiding my surprise, I journeyed on, rubbing her clit gently as the throbbing within her intensified.

Still she kept a straight face, all except for her dazzling blue eyes filling up faster than an Olympic-size pool with pure desire. There was a conversation going on without words, because her body was definitely talking to me. I continued to rub her clit while slowly parting her pussy lips with only the tip of my middle finger, loving how readily her juices moistened my skin.

And still her expression didn't change. It wasn't until I thrust my finger inside her suddenly that I saw her eyes flash like spotlights in search of a suspect. I hadn't expected her to be as tight as she was, though, and when I brought my index finger into that party, her mouth dropped open, allowing a strangled moan to dance off her tongue.

"How long has it been?" I asked, working my fingers at a slow rhythm.

"It's been a-a while," she mumbled, beginning to move with my hand.

I didn't wanna hurt her, but I did want to give her what we both needed. I pulled my fingers out of her long enough to pull her jeans down over her hips, but they got caught up on her boots.

"Hold up a minute, let me —"

"Nah, I got this. Just come here," I said, sliding the driver's seat all the way back and leaning it back as far as it would go.

I pulled her onto my lap until she was sitting on me, facing forward, and then I leaned back with her. Instinct made her put her feet on the steering wheel and use it as leverage as she rose up to take me inside of her. She felt like a virgin, but little by little she opened herself to me until I was completely inside her.

"Gah! Ahmani," she moaned.

"I got you, bae," I whispered, moving both of my hands beneath her sweater and under her bra until I had my hands full with her firm titties.

We moved together with the rhythm of old lovers, giving and taking over and over again. Within minutes I felt her body tense up right before the throws of orgasm rocked her to her very foundation, forcing her to speak in tongues like prophets of old. No sooner had she caught her breath from one wave when there was another there to take her on a ride that left me drenched in her juices and pushing up into her faster and harder.

"Take it. Take this dick!" I demanded, loving the feel of her pussy grabbing at me with each stroke I fed her.

"Oh! Oh, Ahmani! Oh, Ahmani! Oh, Ahmani!" she chanted, bucking against me harder the closer she got to the trifecta she was chasing.

In the moment she came again, I pinched both of her nipples and allowed myself to tumble over the edge with her. I could feel our hearts hammering together as we lay there, synchronized by the race we just ran. I felt her move like she was getting ready to slide back into her seat, but I held onto her tighter, wrapping my arms around her stomach and putting my head on top of hers. This wasn't exactly how I envisioned our first time, but I wanted to savor the flavor of it.

"Can I tell you something?" she asked softly.

"Anything you want."

"My body has never reacted like that."

"You're welcome," I replied, smiling.

"I'm serious, Ahmani. What if – what if I get addicted to you?"

"I'll serve you, don't worry."

"I can't stay here. I can't live with you, your mom, and your brother and sister. Your mom doesn't even like me," she said seriously.

"Sweetheart, it's not that she doesn't like you, she just doesn't know you. And I don't live with her. I've got my own apartment."

"It's not safe for me to even be in Manassas right now. Even when they arrest Aaron, he's gonna still have people looking for me because he knows I'm the only one who can testify against him."

"You've got money, too, and police protection. Fuck that, I'll protect you," I vowed.

"Will you go away with me for a while?"

"Go where?"

"Well, my dad was into real estate, among other things, so we've got different properties in this state and in others."

"I don't know about leaving the state. I mean, I'm on probation now," I replied.

"Well, I've got a spot over near Great Falls, and it's a gated community."

Her offer was enticing, but I'd never lived with a woman before. That was a big deal, and it could fuck up a relationship if the two people weren't ready for that serious step. We had known each other for five minutes, so how were we ready to move in together? At the same time, I couldn't deny the fact I liked her, and the sex was the best I'd ever had.

"If that's what you want, I'm with it."

"It is," she replied, turning to look up at me while pulling me toward her for a kiss. "I'll set everything in motion while you're spending the night at your mom's, and I'll be back to pick you up tomorrow."

"I can have my mom take me to the impound lot to pick up my car, and I can just meet you at your house," I suggested.

"What kind of car do you drive, bae?"

"I got a Honda Accord."

"Let me stop you right there. You're my man now, and I'm not about to have you riding around in a hooptie."

"But I—"

She silenced my intended protest with another kiss, this one deeper and with clear meaning. "No time to argue. It's getting late, and I want another round. Now fuck me."

Aryanna

Chapter Seven

I heard them before I saw them, and I knew what was coming was unstoppable.

"Ahmani!" Keisha yelled as both her and Kendrick hit the corner at full speed and ran toward where I was lying on the couch. It felt like I'd just gotten to sleep minutes ago, but the dream of rest was shattered, because there was no way they weren't about to bug the shit out of me.

"Ow! Watch your knee, Keisha," I said, trying to maintain my breathing despite the two bodies that had pounced on me.

"Where have you been, Ahmani?" Kendrick asked, fighting for position on the upper half of my body.

"I was on vacation," I replied.

"And you didn't take us?" Keisha asked, poking her bottom lip out.

They were fraternal twins, which meant they often wore the same expression, and we all resembled each other in complexion and eye color. Since I didn't have kids of my own, I considered these two my mini-mes. And even though I didn't visit a lot, I tried to show them I loved them.

"I'm sorry, it was a last minute thing for work. I missed you guys, though."

"I'm a girl," Keisha said, hitting me.

"I know what you are, little girl," I replied, tickling her until she scrambled away from me.

"When are you gonna take us somewhere with you?" Kendrick asked.

"Where do you wanna go?"

"I don't know. We never get to go anywhere cool."

"Right now you need to get ready to take your butts to school," my mom said, coming into the living room with a plate in her hand.

"Aw, Mom!" they cried in unison.

All it took was her staring at them to silence their protests, and they were heading in the direction of their bedroom to get ready.

"You still got it," I said, laughing.

"For a few more years, at least. Lord knows how quickly tables turn once puberty rears its ugly head," she replied, handing me the plate of food.

My nostrils flared and my stomach shook like a wet dog as the smell of bacon, eggs, and sausage punched me in the face.

"You cooked for me?" I asked, bewildered.

"Don't sound so shocked. Your brother and sister weren't the only ones who missed you."

I didn't know what to say to that, so the easiest thing to do was pick up my fork and feed my face. My mother's cooking took me back to simpler times in life, happier times I didn't know I was missing.

I'd expected her to go back into the kitchen, but instead she took a seat next to me on the couch. Sleeping on the softness of her large sofa had been a welcome change from what the jail had to offer, but in that moment I was completely uncomfortable sitting there. I didn't know what she planned to say, I just knew she had something to say.

"What's wrong, Mom? I asked.

"What do you mean? Nothing is wrong, now that you're out of that place."

"Okay, but I can tell you've got something on your mind."

"No, I don't, but I forgot your orange juice," she said, getting up and heading back into the kitchen.

The layout of her house had the front door opening into the main hallway that led to the three bedrooms, and directly to the right was the living room. Through the living room was the dining room and kitchen, but from where I sat on the couch I could see into the kitchen. I could see my mother's nervous energy as she moved around, busying her hands with this and that. She definitely had some shit on her mind. I kept eating and I kept watching her, wondering what the hell it could be that had her acting so strange all of a sudden.

"Mom, come here," I called out.

"What is it?" she asked, bringing me a glass of orange juice, but not sitting down again.

"Talk to me for a minute. Come on, sit back down real quick and tell me what's on your mind."

Her hesitation was evident, but she did like that I asked.

"I know you, so I know you don't got no filter when it comes to shit you wanna say. Whatever it is, just say it," I urged.

"I know I don't have the right to meddle in your life, but I don't think it's a good idea to be getting involved with that girl."

"Mom, we're just kickin' it," I replied calmly.

"Is that why you still smell like old sex? I ain't stupid, Ahmani, and neither are you, so don't make decisions without thinking them through. And I don't mean thinking with your dick head, either!"

"Let me ask you a question: what is it exactly that worries you about Katrina?"

"A mother knows," she replied simply.

"I'm gonna need more than that to make an informed decision, don't you think?"

"All I can tell you is what I feel, Ahmani. I almost lost you forever because of something that happened to her family, and I don't want you caught up with any more bullshit that don't concern you."

Looking into her eyes, I saw the fear I thought I heard in her voice was real. I wasn't used to this from my mother, the overprotectiveness. On the one hand I was wondering where it had come from, while on the other hand I could hear the whispers in the back of my mind asking is she was right. Things were moving fast between me and Katrina, but maybe that was because our conversations were so real. I wouldn't know exactly how real it was, though, unless I continued to see this thing through.

"I understand you're concerned, Mom, but I promise you I'm going into this thing with my eyes wide open. Trust me, the mistakes I made with Elyse are still fresh in my mind."

"I can't live your life for you, son, and I haven't always done the right thing, but I always have and always will love you," she said sincerely.

"I love you, too, Mom," I replied, leaning over and kissing her on the cheek.

"Mom, we don't wanna go to school," Kendrick declared, coming into the living room holding our sister's hand.

I admired the tactic of presenting a united front, but they obviously didn't know whom they were fucking with.

"Are y'all gonna make me repeat myself?" my mother asked, smiling despite the implied threat in her tone and the question.

"But Mom, we wanna spend time with Ahmani," Keisha whined.

I couldn't hide my smile because their hand was well-played, but I knew all too well our mother didn't budge on matters of education. I knew I had to step in before they got their asses whooped and still had to go to school.

"You two know the rules: there's no missing school unless you're sick. And before you try to fake like something is wrong with you, I'll make both of you a deal. If you're on your best behavior, starting with no more talk about not going to school, I'll take you to Chuck E. Cheese this weekend."

"Yeah!" they screamed, jumping up and down.

"Now go finish getting dressed," my mom ordered. They disappeared like smoke, chanting "Chuck E. Cheese" the whole way.

"You better not be lying to them."

"Come on, Mom, you know me better than that," I replied, going back to my food.

"After I get them on the bus, I'll take you to get your car."

"It's okay. Katrina is gonna pick me up as soon as I call her."

"Oh. Well, what are your plans after that?" she asked.

"I don't know, honestly. I need to figure out where my life goes now that I'm making major changes."

"What type of changes, Ahmani?"

"What happened was a wake-up call for me. I can't keep living like I was, so now I gotta find out how I survive out here in these streets."

"Well, you know you can always stay here for a while, if you need to," she offered nonchalantly. The fact she actually presented her home as a temporary solution told me how bad my experience had scared her.

"I appreciate that, Mom, but I'm good. I promise. Besides, I know I'm too old and too independent to live under your roof."

"I wouldn't be unreasonable, fool."

I tried to hold my laughter in, but I couldn't because we both knew she was full of shit.

"Just for that, make sure you do the dishes when you're done eating," she said, hitting me upside the head before getting up and heading in the direction my brother and sister had gone.

I finished up my food and orange juice, and then took my plate to the kitchen to do as I was told. I couldn't remember doing dishes in my mother's house since I was about ten years old, so it was kinda funny to me to come full circle.

Before I could finish, the twins dashed in and gave me a hug before they left with our mom for school, reminding me of my promise about Chuck E. Cheese. I didn't need reminding; I knew how much they were looking forward to a day of fun and games. With the dishes done, I went back into the living room to make sure my phone had completely charged, glad I'd gotten my mom the same phone as me last Christmas, which allowed me to use her charger.

It was wild how many texts and missed calls I had, given the fact the world knew I was locked up. Most were expressing disbelief or showing support, but others were calling me everything except the name my mother gave me. When I checked my Facebook page, I found more of the same, but also a surprising message from Elyse wanting me to call her whenever I had someone check my page and relay the message. I couldn't imagine what the hell she thought we had to talk about. After sending Katrina a text to come pick me up whenever she got herself together, I sent Elyse one asking her what she needed.

I'd expected Katrina to still be asleep because she got in later than I did, but her response was immediate, and she said she was on her way. It would've been nice to grab a shower, except I knew if I did I'd have to take the time to clean the whole bathroom once I was done. For that type of hassle, I'd just wait until I got to my apartment.

Within ten minutes I got another text from Katrina telling me she was out front. I made sure to lock the door behind me on my way out, but when I got to the parking lot I didn't see her Jeep Wrangler anywhere.

"You just gonna stand there all day, or are you coming with me?" she asked, climbing out of an all-white Bugatti Veyron.

"I was looking for your Jeep, but I can ride in this."

"Ride in it? You know where we're going, so you drive," she said, walking around to the passenger side of the car.

The Bugatti had my attention until I caught sight of her in that form-fitting black Ralph Lauren sweat suit with the black and gold Gucci sneakers. She knew I was looking, too, because she was throwing that ass hard as she walked.

"You ain't gotta tell me twice," I replied, stepping to the driver's side and getting behind the wheel.

"Good morning," she said, putting her arm around my neck and pulling me toward her.

Our kiss carried the same passion it had hours ago when we'd parted ways, making me wonder if it would always be like this.

"You got here quick," I said, loving how she smelled like sweet peaches.

"I only managed to get an hour's sleep before I was up again."

"Really? Then I must not have done my job properly," I replied, putting the car in gear and pulling off.

"Oh no, you did. And trust me, if you hadn't I would've told you straight up. I'm guessing you didn't see the news this morning, though. They went to arrest Aaron at daybreak, and he didn't go quietly, which resulted in him catching four bullets to the chest."

"So, he's dead?" I asked.

"I wish. No, the last I heard he was still unconscious at Fairfax Hospital, but he's officially in police custody."

"That should make you feel a little better, babe."

"What makes me feel better is knowing you're by my side to protect me from any- and everything," she said, taking my hand in hers and lacing our fingers together.

"I got your back, baby."

"I almost forgot to tell you, you were officially cleared on the news this morning, too. The police commissioner herself made a statement exonerating you."

This revelation brought a smile to my face, because it wasn't every day the cops had egg on their faces. I knew the only reason they made a statement for the press was because this was a case involving a prominent white family, but if it had been some nobody, I would've been pushed out a side door unceremoniously.

"I know she was mad as shit about that," I said, reaching in my hoodie pocket for my ringing phone.

Immediately I recognized Elyse's number and hit the ignore button before putting the phone back in my pocket.

"Who was that?" she asked in what I'm sure she thought was a natural tone. I heard something different, though.

"Nobody."

"Am I delusional, or didn't I just see you hit the ignore button on your phone?" she asked.

"Yeah, you did. And what I meant is it's nobody important."

"When a guy says that, it's usually another bitch on the other end of that call." She was not longer trying for a neutral tone. It was clear she was making a run for pissed, and that was what I didn't need.

"It's my ex, Elyse, but I don't wanna talk to her right now," I replied calmly.

"Right now? Why would you wanna talk to that bitch at all? If it's really over between you two, then there's nothing left to be said. Did you call her?"

"No, I sent her a text and asked what she needed because she sent me a message through my mom for me to get in touch with her while I was locked up" I said, hoping jealousy and insecurity weren't a package deal with this relationship.

We rode in silence for a while, but she never let go of my hand, which I took as a sign she wasn't too pissed off. Elyse was no threat to her, but I had the feeling me saying that wouldn't help in the slightest, so I just left it alone.

"You and I are together."

"Was that a question or a statement?" I asked, smiling. A quick glance at her revealed she wasn't smiling.

"We're together, Katrina."

"So how would you feel if I had men, or an ex-boyfriend, calling my phone?"

"I wouldn't like it," I replied, stating the obvious and knowing where this conversation was headed.

"I told you from the jump that even if I'm just kickin' it was a dude, I'm exclusive. And we're way past kickin' it, so —"

"Baby, relax. I don't want Elyse, and I'm only interested in you, so you don't have to give me a speech on exclusivity. Do I need to swear a blood oath or something?"

"Maybe," she replied with a slight smile.

I was just happy knowing her lips could curl upward at all by this point. I'd been maintaining the speed limit as we maneuvered through the city, but once I got on Route 66 I allowed myself a moment of recklessness. Throwing all caution to the wind, I pressed down hard on the accelerator and let the car do what it was built for. My apartment was in Centreville, which was normally about a twenty-minute drive, but in that Bugatti we got up to 130 miles per hour, and within three minutes I was at my exit.

"Damn, this thing moves," I said, feeling the adrenaline racing through my body.

"Wait until you try out my Porsche."

"How many cars do you have?" I asked curiously.

"I thought I told you, my dad has a collection of automobiles."

I didn't recall that, but it fit right in with their wealth. And as long as she wasn't endangering herself when she switched vehicles, I had no reason to worry. I glanced over at her and asked, "Do you still wanna go to your place near Great Falls? I mean, dude is shot up in the hospital right now."

"He's got friends, Ahmani, and they've got long memories to go with their motivation," she replied.

I didn't know these people, but she did, which meant I couldn't downplay the danger of her situation. I felt like she'd be safe with me wherever we were because my motto was a line from a Tupac song: I ain't no killer, but don't push me. She saved my life, and I'd return the favor.

"I can protect you here, too, you know," I said as we entered my apartment complex.

Lee Overlook Apartments wasn't exactly the projects, but it wasn't upper class condos either. I guess I could best describe it as the gray area in between, where tenants were made up of thieves, the occasional hooker, and functioning addicts of all substances. It was a melting pot mixture, but we seldom saw the police down here because we took care of our own.

"I'm sure you'll protect me anywhere, but there's a new comfort in life I want you to get used to," she replied, stroking the side of my face gently.

For a second I felt like a gigolo, and that turned me on because I had no problem laying pipe for a living. I pulled up in front of my building and we got out.

"I gotta run to the rental office and get a key, wait right here."

"There's no need for that. I've got your keys," Elyse said.

Chapter Eight

It never really mattered how much time passed before coming face-to-face with an ex, especially if the breakup was ugly, because no one is ever prepared. No one is prepared for their presence, their beauty, or the merry-go-round of emotions as their past steps into their present.

When Elyse had first spoken, she was still in the shadows of the building hallway, but now she was walking toward us. Her brown hair was twisted into one long braid that rested on her shoulder, and her smoking gray eyes shown with that intelligence I remembered. The yellow and white sundress she had on was supposed to fit her loosely, but Elyse had curves that wouldn't be denied. To top it off, she had that effortless walk models were known for, with enough sway in her hips to let everyone know that ass was fat in the back. I felt my dick jump involuntarily, and it made me mad she still had this kind of effect on me.

"Why do you have my keys?" I asked.

"I got them from your mom because I needed to pick up some things I'd forgot. But don't worry, I didn't steal anything."

"Were you two living together? Katrina asked, looking at me.

"No, but she spent the night on occasion."

"There were a lot of occasions," Elyse said, smiling at me.

Out of the corner of my eye I saw Katrina close the distance between us, and I thought she was gonna take my hand until I realized what she was doing. Katrina may not have been from the projects, but she could size a bitch up with the best of them and talk that talk without words.

"What are you doing here now?" I asked Elyse, hoping to avoid any bullshit.

"I'd heard you got out, and I wanted to welcome you home."

"He doesn't need you, bit —"

"Hold up, baby, I got this," I said, cutting off the tongue-lashing Katrina was about to deliver.

"Elyse, let's not play like you and I ended on good terms, or even as friends. You did some foul shit to me, so don't act like you give a fuck now."

"You're right, Ahmani, I did do some foul shit, but you don't know how many nights I cried because I'd lost you. And then when you got locked up, I thought I'd never have a chance to show you how sorry I was for breaking your heart. I'm so sorry, Ahmani."

"Bitch, please," Katrina said with open hostility.

My response should've echoed those exact sentiments, but the fact she was apologizing had me at a loss for words. Elyse wasn't the type to apologize. It just wasn't how she was wired. I guess when you looked like she did, you went through life making excuses instead of taking responsibility for what was done. I was amazed and somewhat intrigued by this seemingly changed woman in front of me, but I wasn't 'bout to let her off the hook just yet.

"You're sorry? Were you sorry when any one of them niggas were blowin' your back out? Were you sorry when you were suckin' dick that wasn't mine? Or are you just sorry you got caught?" I asked.

"Trifflin'-ass," Katrina chimed in.

I saw Elyse's eyes slide in Katrina's direction, and I tensed up because Elyse would smack a bitch if provoked, but she didn't say a word and quickly turned her focus back on me.

"I'm sorry I broke the heart of the only man I've ever loved. I'm sorry I lost my best friend because I was too ashamed to come to you about my faults. I'm not sorry you found out, though, because that was the only thing that forced me to change."

"Change? You've changed?" I asked sarcastically.

"I'm a work in progress, yes, but some things have changed. I'm getting counseling for my issues, and I'll probably be going through that for the rest of my life. It's helping, though. And I haven't so much as kissed anyone else since you and I broke up."

"Yeah, right. Your breath smells like dick from here," Katrina said, snickering.

"One more word, bitch, and I'ma melt you right here," Elyse threatened, taking a step in Katrina's direction.

I'd seen Elyse shoot the fade to niggas before, so I knew it was best she didn't put her hands on Katrina's little ass.

"E, don't do that," I said, stepping in between them.

"You better talk to her, because you know I ain't got no issues fixing her face with my wedge sandals."

"It ain't gonna happen, so just say what you gotta say and leave," I replied calmly.

"Look, can I just talk to you in private for a few minutes? This is between me and you, not us and the new girl."

"There is no you and him, bitch. That's my man," Katrina said confidently.

I could tell this was about to go a totally different direction than what was needed, and the best solution was to separate them. How was I gonna do that, though? I turned my back to Elyse and looked at Katrina, trying to figure out what to say and how to say it. I could tell by the look on her face she didn't give a fuck about being outweighed. She was prepared to get it poppin'.

"Baby, I need you to do me a favor. I need you to give me, like, ten minutes with her," I said softly.

The flash of fire in her eyes turned the normally sapphire blue into a pale glacier-like ice, and it made my spine tingle. I wasn't sure how many sides there were to the diamond I considered her to be, but I was definitely looking at one that was new. She was mad in a big way.

"Please," I said, leaning into her and kissing her soft lips in the hopes of making her smile.

Despite her anger, she opened her mouth to me and put her arms around my neck. I knew part of her was using this moment to rub it in Elyse's face that she had me now, and I was okay with that. Katrina was marking her territory.

"I'll tell you what I'm gonna do. I'm gonna go back to my parents' house and grab a few things to take with us, and while you listen to whatever lame excuses your ex has, you can be packing, too. Okay?" she asked.

"I can do that. And I'll make this up to you later," I replied, kissing her again.

"Oh, I know you will. And make sure that bitch is gone by the time I get back," she said, letting go of me and getting back behind the wheel of her car.

I watched her until she disappeared up the hill, and then I turned back around to face Elyse.

"Keys?" I asked, holding my hand out.

Slowly she pulled her yellow clutch purse from under her arm, opened it, and pulled my house key out.

"You've got ten minutes," I said, taking the key from her hand and leading the way down the flight of stairs to my apartment. It had been so long since I used a key it took a few tries to get it in the lock and get the door open. I'd expected to smell stale air, but it was the familiar fragrance Elyse wore that filled my nostrils instead.

Everything looked the way I left it as I stepped into my living room, despite my meager furnishings. I had a sofa and loveseat that were shit-brown and made of some material I couldn't name, but they were comfortable. My 60-inch flat screen T.V. and my stereo were top-of-the-line, though. I mean, what kinda thief would I be if they weren't? I felt like I was seeing everything with new eyes as I took in my little breakfast nook, kitchen, and dining room.

I kicked off my shoes right by the door, loving how the plush beige carpet felt under my feet. To most people my spot was nothing more than a two-bedroom hole in the wall, but until they'd spent time in a cell listening to a muthafucka snore while smelling his farts, they wouldn't understand why this right here was good living.

"Say whatever you gotta say, Elyse. I've got shit to do," I said, going to the kitchen and grabbing a beer from the refrigerator.

"You've got shit to do, or do you have mistakes to make?"

"What's that supposed to mean?" I asked, coming back into the living room. It hadn't taken her long to make herself at home on my couch.

"You know what it means. Why exactly are you running around with the girl whose family you were accused of butchering?"

"I was cleared of that, remember?"

"Cleared or not, I know damn well you ain't stupid enough to think you can trust that bitch."

"You don't know what you're talking about, Elyse. You got no idea what's going on between me and her, and really it ain't your business," I said, heading toward my bedroom.

"I thought your mom was exaggerating, but clearly you done lost your damn mind."

Her words stopped me mid-stride and made me retrace my steps. "What did you say? When the fuck did you talk to my mom?"

"She's worried about you, Ahmani. I know that's completely out of the ordinary, but a lot of shit changed when you got locked up. None of us were prepared to lose you," she said sincerely.

"Okay, first off, you lost me when you couldn't keep your legs closed. And you know what my relationship has been like with my mom."

"We made some mistakes, Ahmani. We fucked up! Especially me. But I still love you, and so does your mom. Think about it. She knows how ugly our breakup was, but she knows we were best friends and inseparable once. Do you really think she would've called me if she wasn't truly afraid?"

"Afraid of what?"

"That you're gonna make a mistake there's no coming back from!" she yelled in frustration.

I was hearing what she was saying, but it was hard to believe her concern given everything that had happened between us. I couldn't trust her; that I knew for sure.

"I'm living my life, and the best thing you can do is live yours. There's really nothing more to say, so you can show yourself out," I said, walking back up the hallway to my bedroom, taking a long drink from the Heineken bottle in my hand.

I didn't wanna be stressed. I was finally home, and I was free, which was a cause for celebration. Maybe I'd take Katrina on a real date before we went out to her house. Knowing her, she probably had plans for us, but the first thing I needed to do was wash the jail off me A.S.A.P. I sat my beer on the sink before I turned the shower on and stripped down to my boxers. Walking back into my room to grab a washcloth, I froze right outside of my bathroom doorway, my mouth falling open against my will. Not only had Elyse not left, but she was actually standing in the middle of my bedroom wearing nothing except her open-toed wedge sandals.

I couldn't stop my eyes from working their way up her juicy thighs to her almost hairless pussy, and further across her stomach until I was locked in on those beautiful double-Ds I remembered. If I concentrated hard enough, I knew I'd remember how her skin tasted, because there wasn't a part of her my tongue hadn't explored. No matter what had happened between us, she was still gorgeous.

"I see you missed me, too," she said, looking pointedly at the opening in my boxers.

"I, uh, I. What are you doing, E?"

"Not what you think I'm doing, although we can after we handle some business."

"What business?" I asked, trying to put my eyes back in my head.

"Well, I knew you wouldn't believe me unless you saw it yourself. I'm pregnant, and it's yours."

Chapter Nine

"You're joking, right?"

"Ahmani, would I play about some shit like that?"

"I don't put nothing past you, slim. And why are you standing there naked, holding a fucking pregnancy test?" I asked, hoping the ringing in my ears would stop.

For a few seconds after she'd said the word *pregnant* my knees locked up, and I thought I was looking at her underwater. If the little voice in my head hadn't reminded me how much of a liar she was, the odds were good I would've hit the floor and been staring at the back of my eyelids. It was obvious she'd gotten naked in front of me to try to distract me from the bullshit coming out of her mouth.

"It should be obvious what the pregnancy test is for, fool, and I'm naked so you can see I'm not hiding nothing."

"Hiding something for what?" I asked.

"Okay, I'm gonna say this shit slowly so you understand, so stop looking at my titties and focus for a second. I'm going to go in your bathroom and pee on this stick, and you're gonna watch me do it so there's no questions later. Understand?"

I nodded my head, trying to figure out where all the spit in my mouth had vanished to.

"Do you wanna inspect my pussy before I take the test?" she asked, coming to stand right in front of me.

"I-I, uh, no," I stammered.

She just shook her head and laughed before pushing past me into the bathroom. I watched nervously as she opened the box and pulled out the little stick that always changed everything. Maybe I should've looked away when she squatted over the toilet and started peeing, but I didn't.

"H-how pregnant are you?"

"About three months, give or take a week."

"Okay, so even if that test comes back positive, you want me to believe it is mine? Without a doubt?" I asked seriously.

"You know we never used protection. And I wasn't letting no other muthafucka fuck me raw."

I had nothing nice to say, so I just stared at her with a look that said *bullshit*.

"I'll gladly do a DNA test, but you better apologize when it comes back that you're my baby daddy," she said, setting the pregnancy test on the back of the toilet.

She flushed the toilet and washed her hands, which gave me a look at her round, plump ass. A look I didn't need.

"Y-you can put your clothes back on while we wait on the test results," I said, hoping the sweat I was feeling on my forehead was from the steam of the shower and nothing else.

"What's wrong, Ahmani? You can't handle it? I know that white girl's body ain't better than mine."

I wanted to brag on Katrina's body and how good the sex was, but in this moment I was having a hard time remembering either. My words got lodged in my chest as Elyse walked toward me and stopped right in front of me, her eyes daring me to reach out and take what I wanted.

"I can smell her on you, you know? Was the pussy good, Ahmani? What about the head? Could she take all this?" she asked, reaching into my boxers and pulling my dick out.

There was no way I could give her an answer to any question because I was too busy trying to remember how to breathe.

"You probably tore her little vagina up with this big ol' thing. She can't take it like I can, we both know that. You wanna put it in me now, don't you, Ahmani? I can swear on our unborn child not another man had laid a finger on me since we last made love. It's still yours, Ahmani, all of it. Are you gonna take it?"

As she talked to me, she was slowly stroking my dick with her incredibly soft hands. I wanted to back up, to break the spell she had me under, but I couldn't move.

"I forgive you, Ahmani. I forgive you for fucking that bitch, and I want to prove to you how much I love you and want you back. Nothing matters but us," she said, dropping to her knees.

My mind processed what she was prepared to do, and disbelief had me paralyzed. No woman would willingly suck a nigga's dick knowing he hadn't washed it since he'd fucked someone else. And even as I though that, I watched her take me into her mouth inch-by-inch until my pubic hairs were tickling her lips. She didn't gag, she didn't flinch. She just slowly backed up and repeated the process at the same speed while looking up at me. When she grabbed my hands and put them on her head, I was lost. All I could do was hold on while she blew my mind. I thought after last night I had my wind back, but it wasn't a hot minute before I felt my cum shooting to the back of her throat.

"Mm, you've been eating plenty fruit, I see," she said, standing up and wiping her mouth.

I couldn't believe she'd just done what she did. I couldn't believe I'd just let her do what she did, because I'd sworn to myself I'd never touch her again.

"Surprise, surprise," she said, picking up the pregnancy test and holding it up for me to see.

Sure enough, there were two blue lines, and I knew what that meant without having to look at the box.

"Don't fucking lie to me, Elyse. Is that my baby you're carrying?"

"Yes, Ahmani. I won't bullshit you about something that serious. That would only make you hate me more, and I don't want that," she said, handing me the pregnancy test and walking out of the bathroom.

I stood there for a few minutes, staring at the results blindly, trying to imagine how my life would change now. Would I be a good father? How was that even a possibility when I didn't have a father of my own? And what would my mother say? I threw the stick in the trash, took my boxers off, and got in the shower. The water was hot enough to cook with, but it felt refreshing pounding away at the sudden anxiety I was feeling.

I always thought Elyse would be the mother of my children, and I would be beyond excited about that, but after we broke up all those dreams disappeared. Now it might actually be happening, and I didn't know what the fuck I was supposed to feel.

The only things I knew for sure were that I had to talk to my mom A.S.A.P. and I didn't need to say shit to Katrina until the DNA results came back.

I spent a quick ten minutes in the shower, wanting to get Elyse out of dodge before Katrina came back and round two started. After drying off and putting some fresh boxers on, I grabbed a pair of dark black

Billionaire Jeans and a matching light blue button-up, dressing in a hurry. Just as I'd put my Air Force Ones back on, my phone started ringing. It was on its fifth ring by the time I got it out of my hoodie and saw it was Katrina.

"Hey, baby, where —"

"Ahmani! Ahmani, someone's following me!" she screamed.

"Following you? Where are you?"

"I'm on the highway coming back to your house," she replied, her voice trembling with fear.

"Okay, just stay calm. What kind of car is following you, and how long have they been following you?"

"I don't know what kind of car it is, but I noticed it when I left my neighborhood."

"Listen to me, your car can outrun almost anything, so just —"

"I'm not in the car right now. I'm driving the Jeep," she said with the beginning of panic vibrating in her voice.

"Okay, it's okay, sweetheart. That Jeep has plenty of giddy-up, so I want you to mash that bitch to the floor and get here."

"Stay on the phone with me! Don't hang up!"

"I'm right here, Katrina. I'm not going anywhere, just concentrate on the road."

I could hear the engine rev when she stepped on the gas, and from the sounds of it a muthafucka was gonna need a hemi or better to keep up.

"How far away are you?" I asked.

"I'm almost to your exit."

"Is whoever was following you still there?" I asked, walking out of my bedroom, hoping Elyse was dressed.

"They're still back there, but not as close, and I'm putting distance between us."

"Good, just get here to me, baby," I encouraged, confused that there was no trace of Elyse in my apartment.

I was getting ready to check my spare bedroom when I spotted the note on my dining room table. There would never come a day when I didn't recognize her handwriting, but while I'd been mentally preparing myself for some profession of undying love, I received another surprise. All she had to say was she would see me in six months unless I reached out to her first. I shouldn't have been surprised she left it up to me, because she knew me well enough to know I was too stubborn for her to force my hand. I was glad she wasn't pushing, because I definitely needed time to think.

"I just got off the highway, and I'll be at your house in a few minutes."

"I'll be out front waiting on you," I said, grabbing my key off the table and heading for the door.

I was only in front of my building for two minutes before I caught sight of her Jeep racing down the hill. She didn't even pull into a parking space, just slid to a stop full of smoke and screaming tires and hopped out. I barely had time to put my phone in my pocket before she leapt into my arms and clung to me like a frightened child.

"It's okay, baby. I got you, and you're safe," I said, stroking her back. She didn't say anything, but I felt her body shaking.

"Hold on while I park your Jeep and we'll go inside."

She was reluctant to let me go, but eventually I was able to put her down long enough to get her ride out of the middle of the road.

"Hold on, bae," she said, going to the passenger side and opening the door after I'd already gotten out.

I saw her grab something out of the glove compartment, but she put whatever it was in her sweatpants pocket. We went downstairs and into my apartment, where I fixed her a shot of Henney to calm her nerves, and I took a hit from the bottle because I definitely needed it.

"You okay?" I asked, leading her to the couch.

"Yeah, I think so."

"Tell me what happened."

"I was leaving my parents' house when I noticed a gray sedan behind me. At first I thought I was paranoid so I got on Route 23 and drove toward Georgetown South, thinking heading toward the hood would help weed out regular traffic. The car stayed with me, even when I turned around and headed back through Manassas to get on 66. That's when I got scared."

"Did you see who was in the car?" I asked, pouring another shot into her glass.

"No, but it was a white guy."

"Okay. Let me grab my duffel bag and we'll got on the move," I said, passing her the bottle of liquor.

As soon as I got in my room, I grabbed a bag and started hurriedly tossing my clothes into it, too distracted to worry about the outfits I was choosing. In the front of my mind I was trying to figure out the best way to deal with Katrina's safety issues, but in the back of my mind I kept hearing a baby cry. Fatherhood was forever, so there was really no way to prepare for it.

What had me fucked up was how much my life had changed in twelve hours. I'd gone from incarceration to live-in pussy and a baby on the way! Wait until old man Doug heard about this shit. With my clothes in the bag, I went to the bathroom and grabbed my toiletries before heading back to the living room.

"A'ight, babe, I'm ready to —"

I pulled up short at the sight of her standing by my dining room table with Elyse's note in one hand and a chrome and black Bauer .380 in the other.

"K-Katrina," I said slowly.

"What's this note mean? Why will she see you again in six months?"

Chapter Ten

"Baby, where did you get a gun? And why do you have it out?" I asked, slowly setting my bag down, but never taking my eyes off of hers.

"It's impolite to answer a question with a question, Ahmani. So, tell me why your ex will contact you in six months unless you contact her first."

My mother may not have raised me, but nothing I learned from her or the streets made me a nigga too dumb to see now wasn't the time for keeping shit one hundred. Katrina didn't have a deranged look in her eyes or anything, but that could be her just hiding her loco really well.

"She wants us to remain friends, and I told her that would take time because a lot of damage was done during our breakup. Plus, I needed space to give me and you room to grow and give our relationship a chance."

"And she figured six months was enough time for what we have to run its course?" she asked.

"Honestly, babe, I don't know what she thought because I told her to let herself out of my house and I went to get ready for you."

The look in her eyes said she was weighing my words carefully, but I wasn't panicked. It wasn't like she was pointing the gun at me or anything.

"To answer your questions, the gun was a gift from my father on my eighteenth birthday because he wanted me to be able to protect myself out here on my own. And the reason I have it out is because someone walked past your balcony. I was coming to get you when this note caught my eye."

"I should've had my blinds closed, but it's okay, babe. People walk past all the time," I said, pulling her toward me while taking the pistol from her hand and setting it on the table.

She didn't resist, simply stepped into my embrace and held on tight, and that allowed me to breathe a little easier. For a split second I thought I might've had a live one on my hands, and lord knows I didn't need no crazy bitch to complicate my life even more. No, thank you!

"I'm gonna teach you how to use it," she mumbled into my chest.

"Use what, babe?"

"The gun. I know that's not really your thing, but we don't know what's coming, and I want you to be able to protect yourself and me."

"I'm cool with that, but for now you should probably be the one doing the carrying," I suggested.

"That's fine."

"Okay, so are you ready to go?" I asked, pulling back so I could look down into her beautiful face.

"I was, but now I'm having other ideas."

"Such as?" I asked.

"Well, if I have my way, then it'll be a while before we come back here. Who knows, we might enjoy living together more than either of us is anticipating. My point is, I wanna take some time and leave my mark on your apartment."

"What did you have in mind?" I asked, smiling.

The smile she gave me was sexiness, pure and simple, with a mixture of naughty that already had ideas forming in my head. When she slowly started to unbutton my shirt, I knew we were on the same page. Experience had taught me while sex in a car was very much enjoyable, it was still constricting because of the limited space. We had a whole apartment to get down with, and it was my goal to take both of our minds off Elyse.

It only took moments before there were no more clothes in between us and I had her up on the dining room table. I was just about to dive in when I saw Elyse's note and a voice in my head screamed for me to get a condom.

"Hold on, baby, let me go grab something."

"Un-uh, whatever it is can wait," she replied, grabbing my dick and pulling me toward her.

"C-condom," I moaned right before she locked her legs around my back and pulled me inside her.

"I-I'm on the p-pill."

I know some chicks lie about shit like that, but at that point I had to give her the benefit of the doubt, because I was not climbing out of the pussy. I knew in her mind she thought she could take whatever I was gonna give her, but as I began giving her them long, pounding strokes, I could see the shock all over her face.

"I'ma m-make you mine," I told her.

When she opened her mouth to speak, I fucked her harder until the thought of words was long forgotten.

I spent the next two hours giving Katrina the grand tour of my apartment, making sure not to miss a room on our travels. She hadn't been a virgin, but I could tell she damn sure hadn't experienced what I was giving her, and she was loving it. When I elected to show her the softer side of being with me, I'd almost panicked because she'd started crying in the middle of it. I froze, asking her again and again if I was hurting her, but she swore I wasn't and begged me to keep going. I gave her what she asked for until she finally tapped out.

"Are you ever going to feed a bitch, or are you just gonna fuck me until my pussy doesn't work anymore?"

"You asked for it," I replied, laughing.

"Maybe I did, but now I'm asking for food."

"Do you wanna take a shower first?" I asked, getting out of bed.

"Nope, I wanna smell like you. And I want you to do the same," she said, following my lead. Hand-in-hand, we went back into the dining room and got dressed.

"I'ma take you back to my mom's real quick and have her whip up some good home cooking for lunch," I said, picking up my duffel bag.

"Or we could try something normal, like going to a restaurant. Unless you're ashamed to be out in public with me."

"Katrina, why would you even think some shit like that? Stop acting like you don't know you're a bad bitch who turns heads everywhere," I said, gently pushing some of her hair behind her right ear.

"I'm glad you think so. It's just that, well, whatever is happening between us didn't start the way one normally approaches a relationship. I'm not saying that's a bad thing, I just wanna do stuff regular couples do."

"You're right. Nothing about how we got to this point is normal by any stretch of the imagination, but that only makes our story more interesting. As for doing shit like regular folk, how about we grab lunch wherever you like and then we do a little grocery shopping so I can cook you dinner?"

"You cook?" she asked.

"Why do you seem shocked? I've more-or-less been on my own since I was fourteen, and you don't get a body like this by starving."

"You do have a nice body," she said, putting both of her hands on my chest and rubbing.

"Thank you, but if you wanna make it out of this apartment, I suggest you stop rubbing on me."

Reluctantly she put her hands up in surrender, but her smile promised we were only finished for the moment. "A'ight. I'll feel safer out in public with you by my side," she decided.

"Grab your gun and let's go," I said.

I locked up my apartment and we made our way to her jeep, making sure to keep our eyes open for anyone lurking. I'd just thrown my bag in the back and hopped in the passenger seat when my phone started ringing. Out of the corner of my eye I saw Katrina flinch, and I prayed it wasn't Elyse calling to fuck up my mood. I didn't know the number, but I answered anyway, and as soon as I did I smiled.

"Who is it?" Katrina asked.

"My nigga from inside," I said, pressing zero to connect our call.

"Old nigga!"

"What up, young boy? I see you really out there in the world," old man Doug said.

"Yeah, pops, it wasn't no fluke shit. I'm out here. How you holding up?"

"You know how it is in here: same shit, same toilet, and a whole lot of whispers now that you're gone. Bitch-ass niggas!"

"Don't let that shit stress you, old man. They talked about Jesus, so why wouldn't they talk bad about me? I don't want you in there getting caught up with the bullshit, trying to defend my name," I said sternly.

"It's all good, young nigga, it's all good. Did you meet up with ol' girl?"

"Man! She was waiting for me out front," I told him, feeling Katrina's eyes on me.

"Oh yeah? Did she look as good as you remembered?"

"Nah, better. Way better!" I replied, laughing at the questioning look she was giving me.

"I bet she put that pussy on you good, too!"

"Uh, that's a convo for later on, pops."

"Oh, she must be right next to you, then," he said laughing.

"You better know it."

"A'ight, well, I just wanted to check on you, but I won't hold you up. You be safe out there, and take your time," he said.

"Listen, I've got some moves to make to get my living arrangements situated, but I want you to call me tonight. I'm on the move right now, so I'll get a money order and drop it off at the jail personally."

"You ain't gotta do that."

"Shut up, old man. I got you, and that's the end of it. Check your account when the shift changes," I said, signaling Katrina to start the Jeep so we could move out.

"I appreciate it, my nigga, truly."

"I appreciate you and everything you did for me while I was in there. I ain't never gonna forget it. Call me later."

"I will," he replied before hanging up.

"You made a friend while you were inside?" Katrina asked.

"Something like that. Facing a life sentence can take a lot out of a muthafucka, but he helped me keep my mind right and stay focused. Most niggas wouldn't have gave a damn or would've tried to use my situation to their advantage, but old man Doug wasn't like that. He was a real one."

"Sounds like a rare thing, especially in that environment."

"As rare as a unicorn," I said, hoping one day I'd be able to repay him for all he'd done for me.

"So, where are we going first?" she asked.

"I gotta make a stop and pick up some money that's owed to me so I can put a few dollars on the old man's books."

"You don't gotta do that."

"What do you mean?" I asked.

"Whatever money somebody owes you, they can keep it. Your old life and the people in it need to be things of the past if you wanna avoid going to prison. I know you're an independent person who's had to survive out here, but you're worth more than money to me. So, until you find something that you're good at legally, I got you."

"Katrina, I —"

"No part of that was a request. Now just sit here and look pretty," she said, pulling up in front of the bank and hopping out.

I did like what I was told, using the time to go on Facebook and see what was shaking. There was no way to catch up on everything I'd missed, but there was no way not to go on Facebook, so I just had to get in where I fit in.

I Instagrammed a shot of me in the Jeep so the streets would know the rumors were true, that a nigga was back. Normally I wouldn't do some shit like that with my beard looking rough and my hairline not crisp, but the struggle was real, and I wanted to convey that. As soon as I posted it, I had a flood of messages in my DM, and everybody was screaming "welcome home" all over my page. I appreciated the love, and as I was scrolling through my page, I saw I hadn't been as forgotten as I'd felt.

"A'ight, so do you wanna swing by the jail first, or go eat?" Katrina asked, getting back behind the wheel.

"I better feed you before shit gets ugly. But sweetheart, you don't gotta give my people's no money. Me picking up what's owed to me and dropping him some off ain't a big deal."

"It's sweet that you still think this is up for discussion, but we should really decide where we're gonna eat," she said, pulling away from the bank.

"How about Cracker Barrel?"

"They do have some good food there. Okay. Let's drop this money off first, though, so when we leave we can go straight to the store and then home," she said.

"We gotta go get a money order, then."

"No, we don't. I got a cashier's check in the bank," she replied, digging it out of her pocket and passing it to me.

When I first glanced at it, I thought she was being too generous, but when I really looked at it, I saw she'd lost her damn mind.

"This can't be real," I said.

"Of course it's real. Why would you say that?"

"Because there's no way you're giving him five grand! I mean, who does that?"

"Baby, it's not a big deal. It was obvious from your conversation with him and what you told me that you're fond of the old man. If he's your friend, then he's our friend. Plus, I know you told him about me," she said, smiling.

"Yeah, but we just talked about —"

"I know you didn't say anything bad. The fact I was on your mind at all is what matters."

"How could you not be on my mind? Even before I knew who you were your letters had my attention because you were showing me someone still cared. I admit I thought you were bat-shit crazy a time or two, but overall I was still happy every time I got a letter."

"Do you know how long I've waited to have a real conversation with you?" she asked, looking over at me.

"No."

"Ever since that night at the party. I mean, I've seen you since then at different parties, but I never had the nerve to talk to you."

"The nerve? What were you scared of? I'm just a regular nigga," I said, taking her hand in mine.

"You're far from a regular muthafucka. I didn't go to Stonewall Jackson High with you because my parents insisted on private school, but I still knew who you were. You've always been popular, Ahmani."

"And you're not? I don't care what school you went to, because there's no way every dude wasn't trying to holla at you."

"All they wanted was sex. And I've got a bad habit of choosing the wrong guys," she said softly.

I didn't know all that lurked behind that statement, but the pain was evident on her face, even from the side. There were layers to Katrina, that much was obvious, but I wondered if she was willing to let me in and get to know her fully. I decided to take the slow approach so I wouldn't spook her, and we just kept the conversation light as we dropped the money off, and then went to eat.

Despite the fact we'd had animal sex already, we still saw this as our first date, and we treated it as such without all the nervousness. We laughed and joked, and she brought me up to speed on what she'd been getting into over the past few years.

Eventually the conversation turned to our exs, but hers led in a different direction because it concluded with tragedy. She hid it well. It was still plain to see her parents' death was something she'd always struggle with. I didn't think she would allow me to comfort her in public, but I still got up and sat in the chair next to her and put my arm around her. I felt bad for a lot of reasons, and I felt a certain amount of guilt, too. I couldn't change our pasts though; I could only pray the future was brighter.

Chapter Eleven

Katrina's house had been something out of a travel magazine, which shouldn't have been a surprise, but I'd be lying if I said it wasn't. It was one of only three positioned on a cul-de-sac, and we had to pass through a fifteen-foot black wall with a wrought iron gate to gain access to it. Secluded didn't begin to describe it.

The mini mansion had six bedrooms, five baths, a private gym, a media room, and an outdoor in-ground pool. When we pulled into the three-car garage, I saw the black-on-black Porsche 911 Katrina had told me about, and a burgundy H2 hummer sitting on twenty-eight-inch spiders she'd forgotten to mention. I didn't even have time to admire her rides because she was pulling me into the house, and my mind was blown.

The garage led us into the kitchen, which was a chef's playground. It had the finest cooking equipment and plenty of space to maneuver. She dragged me from room to room, across pristine marble floors, showing me priceless works of art by painters like Picasso, Van Gogh, and Leonardo Da Vinci. The first floor of the house looked like a museum, but the second floor had the touches of home that said this place wasn't simply a trophy. There were pictures of Katrina and her parents throughout different stages of her life, some vacation scenes or adventures, and a couple school pictures with her missing a few teeth. Coming from where I did, I really didn't think I could ever make myself at home like Katrina wanted me to, but she wouldn't take no for an answer.

After she shared half a bottle of some really old — but really good — wine, I wasn't trippin'. I set up shop in the kitchen and went to work on our meal, blowing her mind with the fact I hadn't been frontin' about my skills. I whipped up some fried pork chops, mashed potatoes, and green beans, but I let Sarah Lee handle the dessert because my baking game was suspect. I'd thought after indulging in some good food and getting a little more tipsy we'd christen the house the same way we did my apartment, but somehow we ended up talking. We discussed everything from life in the projects to politics, and none of it seemed forced or boring. It had been a long time since I'd really sat down and picked a female's brain like that, and it was a pleasant surprise to find someone I had so much in common with.

Of course, that turned my thoughts to Elyse because she was the only other woman I'd felt this comfortable with. Katrina was refreshing, though, and not as complicated as I thought she might be. Part of me wondered if I was being judged by her for the shit I'd done, but I never got that vibe. Before I knew it, the sun had set and risen again, and we were still cuddled together on her white leather sofa, kickin' it.

"Can you believe we've been up all night?" I asked, stoking her hair.

"I can believe it. I just can't believe we've been talking and not doing other things."

"Talking is just as important as those other things," I said, kissing her behind her left ear.

"Agreed. I've never been able to talk to a man like I do you. Hell, I've never had one listen to me like you."

"I can't learn about you if I don't listen to you more. Besides, I think you're interesting and not as stuck up as some pretty little rich girls."

"Thanks," she said, laughing and giving me a slight jab with her elbow.

"You know I'm joking. So, what do you have planned for today?"

"I don't know. I thought we'd start with making love all over the house and see where that takes us," she replied, grinding her ass on me suggestively.

"As tempting as that sounds, I've gotta go to my mom's house for a little while."

"Do you gotta go to your mom's every day? Is it mandatory that you check in before getting some pussy?"

"What are you talking about? I just told my brother and sister I'd take them to Chuck E. Cheese," I said, bewildered at her attitude change.

"Whatever, Ahmani. It seems like every five minutes you gotta go to your momma's house for some reason or another. Maybe you should've lived with her."

"Okay, first off, I don't need to live with no-damn-body because I got my own shit. It may not be a mansion like you're used to, but I'm good with it. And I'm only here because you asked me to be. And number two, you of all people should know how important it is to spend time with your family when you have the chance."

"Whatever, Ahmani. Take the car or truck and go do what you gotta do," she said, unfolding from our embrace and walking out of the room.

Had we really just had out first fight because I was going to spend a few hours with my family? It didn't seem possible to me that we would argue over some dumb shit, but the fact she wasn't still lying in my arms was all the proof I needed. Shaking my head, I got up off the couch and went upstairs to grab a quick shower and change. The size of the shower in her master bedroom was equivalent to damn near half of my apartment, with a his-and-hers showerhead. I could only imagine how sex would be with Katrina in there, but it looked like that was gonna have to wait.

I spent twenty minutes beneath the relaxing spray, trying to clear my mind before I had enough clarity to get out. I threw on a white Black Billionaire button-up with some matching tan-colored jeans and my butter Timbs and grabbed my phone before heading downstairs. It had been my plan to squash the bullshit with Katrina, but I couldn't find her on my room-to-room search. I'd seen where she'd hung her keys on a pegboard last night, right inside the door to the kitchen that led to the garage. When I went to get the keys to the Hummer, I noticed a set missing.

Walking into the garage, I saw the Hummer against the far wall and the Jeep next to it, but an empty space where the Porsche used to be. Evidently she was madder than I thought. I went back to grab the keys to the truck, and that's when I noticed the stack of $100 bills sitting on the little table right under the pegboard. Was this her way of apologizing? Or was this her way of controlling me?

Keys in hand, I left the money right there, went back to the truck, hopped in, and pulled off. It was obvious me and Katrina were gonna have to sit down and get some shit straight. The only way to eliminate misunderstandings in a relationship was to put all the cards on the table and let it be known what it is.

I could focus on that later, though. Right then I needed to figure out how I was gonna tell my mom Elyse was pregnant. I knew me having a kid at a young age was something she'd worried about since I started slinging dick, so her first response probably wouldn't be joy. I didn't think she'd be too mad, though, because she knew I would always take care of what's mine. It wasn't just on me, it was on Elyse, too. When I got to a stoplight, I pulled my phone out and called her, smiling at the fact I'd obviously interrupted her sleep. I told her to meet me at my mom's in forty-five minutes, and then I hung up before she could get a word out. I was petty as fuck, but I didn't care.

Riding on, I became instantly spoiled with the Hummer and how smooth it was, plus the system knocked. Despite what Katrina had said yesterday, I was still my own man, so I felt no guilt when I swung past my nigga Black Boy's house. Black Boy was a dude named Ira, and he was a hustler of all trades, just like me, but the difference was he was the type to rearrange your thoughts with his AK. We'd grown up together in Georgetown South, so he was more like my brother, which was the only reason I'd given him my merchandise without payment.

I knew what I was riding in would attract enough attention niggas would call or text him long before I got to his door, so I wasn't surprised to see him sitting on the hood of his car with his vest on and AK out.

"Still ready for war, huh, my nigga?" I asked, hopping out of the truck.

"You know how it is, bruh. It's good to see your ass out that box. I was wondering when you'd find your way back home."

It was rare for him to smile. It was part of the fear his six-foot, two-inch, 220-pound frame imposed, but he showed me his teeth as he pulled me in for a hug.

"Damn, my nigga, did you get darker?" I asked, dodging his lazy swing as I pulled back.

"Stop hating, nigga. Bitches love this Haitian black skin, and you know it. I took plenty pussy from you."

"Ah, whatever, bruh. Don't lie on your dick."

"He ain't never gonna do that," Amee said, coming toward us from her apartment.

If me and Black Boy were brothers, then Amee was our little sister. We'd all grown up together, but it had been our job to protect Amee from the nothing-ass niggas in the projects who just wanted to use her. Her beauty was undeniable because she was a five-foot, one-inch redbone with hypnotizing green eyes, and she was thicker than a rainbow. It was rare to find beauty and brains in one package, but I'd lived next door to it almost all my life.

"What's up, little Amee?" I asked, pulling her into my arms and squeezing her tightly.

"It's good to see you. I'd heard you got out. Are you gonna stay your black ass out of trouble this time?"

"Yep, if you let me take you to dinner," I bargained.

"Boy, please. You can put some groceries in the house for me and your little cousin."

No matter how much me and Black Boy had tried to keep boys away from Amee, the heart wants what it wants, and she'd fallen victim to my nothing-ass cousin. The only good thing that came from that was their son.

"How is Isaiah?" I asked.

"As bad as you and his daddy! You need to talk some sense into him."

"I can do that. How have you been holding up?" I asked, pulling back to look into her face.

I knew she was gonna lie to me because she wasn't the type to want pity from anyone, especially those who loved her. She'd rather put on that brave face and suffer in silence, no matter how bad the pain got. For the better part of fifteen years, Amee had suffered from Reflex Sympathetic Dystrophy Syndrome, or more commonly called RSD. For some people, it was called Complex Regional Pain Syndrome, or CRPS. It was all a rare, chronic, progressive condition in which people experienced severe pain, inflammation, and changes in the skin. Some days she couldn't get out of bed because the pain was so bad, and she could never stand for long periods of time. Her life consisted of an agony most would never know or be able to endure, but she took it like a champ.

There was no cure as of yet, which meant all she could do was live with it, and that wasn't easy living. For that reason her strength had always been remarkable to me, and I didn't pity her because I had respect for that strength. The struggle was real, but Amee was realer.

"You know I'm good. I have my days, but what else is new?" she said, giving me a smile that didn't quite reach her beautiful eyes. I knew not to push it, though.

"We all have our days," Black Boy said.

"Preach. I won't even tell you how I done got myself caught up, but quiet as it's kept, you two might be an aunt and uncle real soon," I said.

"Seriously?" Amee asked, giving me a genuine smile.

"Yeah, that's what it looks like, but I won't know until the DNA test gets done."

"I ain't trying to be the uncle. Make me the godfather," Black Boy requested.

"Yes, Godfather," I said in my best Marlon Brando impersonation.

"Who's the baby mama?" Amee asked.

"Elyse."

My response earned me silence accompanied by some very loud looks. Once we'd broken up I'd had to tell my fam what the business was, so the looks they were giving me right now were understandable.

"I'm on my way to my mom's to break the news to her," I said, stepping back from Amee.

"Good luck with that," Black Boy said sarcastically. He knew what my relationship with her was like, which meant the potential for disaster was high.

"You two gonna get back together?" Amee asked.

"Nah, it ain't nothing like that. Plus, I got a new squaw."

"Oh yeah, chief tender dick? Who you booed up with now?" Black Boy asked.

"You don't know her," I replied nonchalantly.

The look he gave me easily translated into "Nigga, please" because we both knew Manassas was his city, and there weren't too many bitches he didn't know.

"Her name is Katrina," I said.

"Where she from?" Amee asked.

"My nigga, I know you ain't talkin' about the white girl whose parents you was accused of knocking off," Black Boy said, getting up off the hood of his Mustang.

I figured he might have known her, but the speed with which he'd put shit together was startling.

"How did you —"

"Because I watch the news, nigga, and because I know you think with your dick with the best of them. I ain't trying to judge you because you my dude regardless, but be careful because I got mixed reviews on her."

"What do you mean?" I asked.

"When I seen you was accused of making her disappear, I went to the street to find out what type of chick she was. Rich white girls love to party in the hood, and I figured that's where your paths might've crossed for you to be able to pick her spot to hit. Some muthafuckas I asked said she was cool, and others said she was shaky, but everybody said she's stingy with that pussy. Don't catch no rape case," he told me seriously.

"Never would I, and trust me, she ain't as stingy as you think," I replied, smiling.

"You so nasty," Amee said, laughing.

"He lyin'," Black Boy declared.

"When you ever known me to lie on my dick, bruh?"

He didn't say shit because we both knew neither one of us had to do that. "Just be careful, my nigga," he said, pulling out his phone and checking his messages. "Look, I gotta make a move, but here. And welcome home." He passed me a knot of folded-up bills.

I wouldn't insult him by counting it because I knew he'd looked out with more than what he owed me. We gave each other dap, and then he disappeared around a corner. When I was sure he was gone, I peeled off $300 and put it in Amee's hand.

"No, Ahmani, don't do that. We're good," she protested.

"Take it or I'm gonna stick it in your bra and cop a feel while I'm doing it."

"Yeah, and I'll beat your ass, nigga."

"I love you, too, Amee. I'll be back to see you and the little man soon," I said, giving her a hug and a kiss on the forehead before getting back in the Hummer. I waited until she got back into the house before pulling off and heading toward my mom's.

By my calculations, Elyse should've been pulling up at the same time I did, but when I got there her dark green Jeep Cherokee was already parked and the hood was cold. When I got up to the door, I didn't even have a chance to knock before my mom pulled the door open.

"Took you long enough," my mom said.

"Good morning to you, too, Mom."

"It would've been a good morning if your black ass hadn't woke us up early."

"What do you mean?" I asked, closing the door and following her into the living room.

What I saw when I got there had me puzzled at first because I didn't understand why my alleged baby mama had come out of the house in her pajamas. As I focused on her lack of make-up, messy hair, and bare feet, it become clear she didn't come out of the house this way. She'd slept there.

"Mom, what the hell is going on?" I asked as calmly as I could.

"From what Elyse said, you know what's going on. She's pregnant."

Chapter Twelve

"What part of your brain tol' you it would be a good idea to tell my mom about you being pregnant before I could? I mean, damn, could you not wait a fucking day? Or were you that thirsty for sympathy that —"

"Ahmani, stop. She didn't come here and tell me she was pregnant after she told you. I've known for about a month now," my mom confessed, sitting next to Elyse on the couch and taking her hand.

I had so many words on the tip of my tongue I thought I might scream hysterically, but I took a moment to pull my shit together. "Why didn't you tell me? I called you at least once a week when I was inside. You had plenty of opportunities to tell me, or at the very least you could've told me to call Elyse."

"I told your mom I wanted to be the one to tell you, and I would've as soon as your trial was over. Ahmani, I can't imagine exactly what you were feeling and dealing with every day in there, but I really didn't wanna add stress to your life — especially after the way I hurt you. I figured waiting until the trial was over would allow you to focus on defending yourself, and the baby would probably be born, so we could get the DNA test done."

"He doesn't need no DNA test," my mom said.

"The hell I don't!" I replied quickly.

Because of the relationship my mom had with Elyse, I hadn't gone into specific details about our breakup, but if she thought I wasn't getting a DNA test done, she was trippin'.

"I don't have a problem with a DNA test, Ms. Tamika. In fact, I want to do it so there will never be any questions and he can never throw the past in my face," Elyse said, looking defiantly at me.

"Ain't no need to bring up the past because what's done is done. Besides, you said Ahmani was the last man you slept with, so —"

"Wait, you told my mom what happened?" I asked, stunned.

"I had to. I couldn't just show up on her doorstep pregnant and not answer the questions she had."

I didn't even know what to think about that or what to say. The woman I met and fell in love with didn't have honesty issues, but after her double life came to light, I didn't think she was capable of telling the truth. The only thing I knew right then was I obviously didn't know who Elyse was.

"So, you're okay with the idea of me being a father?" I asked.

"I'm okay with the idea of me being a grandmother. I hope you'll be a good father, but if you're not, I'm prepared to show Elyse how to be a strong single mother."

"If that baby is mine, I'll be a good father."

"The baby's yours, Ahmani. I swear on a stack of bibles," Elyse said.

It was on the tip of my tongue to tell her what I thought of her odds for spending eternity in Hell already, but the look in her eyes was to genuine.

"So, are you living here now?" I asked.

"Well, I was staying at your apartment, but with you coming home, I knew I had to give you your space."

"What happened to your apartment?"

"Times got hard. After we broke up, I did a complete overhaul on my life and got away from everything and everyone that wasn't good for me. It's been rough, but I didn't like who I was, so I changed."

I didn't know if she was laying all this on me to make me sympathetic toward her, I just knew it was working.

"You can go back to my apartment and stay there," I offered.

"She's fine here, Ahmani. And besides, you two living together might not be —"

"He's not staying there," Elyse interjected.

I could see her doing the math in her mind and putting it together with everything that had happened yesterday, and for some reason I felt guilt.

"What do you mean, he's not staying there?" my mom asked, looking back and forth between us.

To her credit, Elyse didn't say shit, but I knew that was only because she wanted to enjoy my mom blowing my shit back.

"I'm staying with Katrina because —"

"You're what?" my mom asked in that overly-polite tone everyone identified as the calm before the storm.

"Mom, just listen to me before you start trippin'. The guy responsible for what happened to Katrina's parents has a long reach, and she doesn't feel safe by herself."

"And why are you the dumbass who has to make her problems your problems?"

"Mom."

"'Mom' my ass, Ahmani! I didn't raise you to be a dummy or a bulletproof vest. If that bitch is scared, then tell her to hire a bodyguard, but it ain't no way you should be putting your life on the line for someone you just met!"

"She saved my life, Mom. I'd still be sitting in that funky-ass jail if she hadn't come forward."

"So, are you fucking her out of pity?" my mom asked, disgusted.

"It doesn't matter why I'm fucking her. It's my decision and my dick!"

"Nigga, what?" my mom said, shooting up off the couch like her ass was on fire. She may have only been five foot, four inches and 140 pounds soaking wet, but she was a brawler, and the look in her eyes said we were about to rumble.

"Fuck you think you talking to?" she asked, advancing around the coffee table in my direction.

"All I'm saying, Mom, is if me being with Katrina is a mistake, it's my mistake, and I'll learn from it."

"If you live long enough to learn anything! Your head is so far in that bitch's pussy already, I doubt you can find your way out. But you better keep one thing in mind: Elyse is carrying your baby, and that baby deserves to know its father. You can't do a damn thing from your grave," she said, grabbing her purse and car keys off the table and brushing past me.

I started to ask her where she was going, but Elyse shook her head and mouthed 'no' to keep me from speaking. The door opened and then slammed hard enough to shake the entire apartment, leaving me and Elyse staring at each other in silence. I was a grown-ass man who didn't like to be told what to do, but I understood my mother's worry on some level. There really did seem to be some truth to what Elyse had said about my incarceration changing everybody.

"You wanna give me a lecture, too?" I asked, sitting down on the opposite end of the couch from her.

"That's not my place. As someone who has loved you for a long time, I will ask you to be certain, because I think our child will be better off growing up with you in their life."

"It's still hard to believe you're pregnant. I mean, I know we never used condoms, but you were getting that shot."

"Yeah, I was. Until I wasn't."

"Huh?" I asked, looking at her closely.

"I was getting my shot on the regular, but I stopped," she replied softly.

"W-why would you do that? Why didn't you tell me?"

"I wanted a child. I wanted your child, but I didn't know how you would feel about that."

"So you thought you'd just spring it on me? That's bullshit, slim!"

"I'm not saying I was right for the way I did it, but our child was created in love, Ahmani, and that's what matters."

"Love? How can you sit there and say you loved me when you were fucking other niggas?" I asked, feeling the old anger at her betrayal rising within me.

"Even pretty girls are insecure, Ahmani. That's on me. I won't make excuses for the shit I did because there are none, but the truth is I didn't love myself enough, and I'm getting the help I need to work through that. I always loved you, though, as much as I was capable of loving. I may not have thought I was good enough for you, but I loved you anyway."

"Not good enough? What are you talking about?"

"You're a good man, Ahmani. You have your flaws, but you've always been kind, generous, honest, and a gentleman. When I first got here, everybody was coming at me, trying to holla, and all of them were so blinded by my looks they didn't realize I was watching who was watching me. You were the one who got my attention because I saw how both men and women reacted to you. You got love and respect, and a man who got plenty of that could only be one with good character. So, I gave you a shot. Or at least that's what I told myself, but really I was hoping you'd be the one to save me."

"Save you? From what?"

"From myself. The truth is my mother and father were married, but there was no love there. Because of that, my dad was hardly around, so I went looking for love in other places, and I found the illusion of it easily because of how I looked. Needless to say, I lost my virginity at eleven years old and never looked back. My parents didn't notice. They had enough to deal with trying to keep their marriage afloat. I just kinda faded into the background with guys who promised me love for as long as it took for them to cum. You were different, though. You were real. I never told you this, but when you came by my house the night after we first slept together and brought me that teddy bear, I bawled like a baby for hours."

"Why?" I asked, curious as to why something so innocent would reduce her to tears.

"Because it was something so simple, and yet no one had ever done that. I fell in love with you that day, Ahmani, but I couldn't outrun my demons."

For years I had considered Elyse my best friend, my wifey, but I'd just learned more about her in this one conversation than I had in our whole relationship. I wanted to be mad and ask her why she'd hid all of this from me, why she hadn't trusted me enough to be completely honest. The only thing stopping me was the realization it was only through her work in therapy that we were able to speak about this now. I needed to internalize what she was saying and not judge her for it.

"I guess there was a lot I didn't know about you," I said.

"I didn't want you to know, Ahmani. I was just hoping your love could make me whole."

"I'm sorry I wasn't able to do that, E."

"But you were. The reason I haven't done anything with anyone is because all I wanted was you, and no substitutes would work. I know it's crazy, but losing you pushed me over the edge, and I either had to fix what's broken or stay forever shattered."

"Regardless of your motivation, I'm glad you're doing better," I said sincerely.

"I am, except this baby has me horny as fuck all the time," she replied, laughing.

As much as I didn't want to, I smiled, my mind going back to how insatiable she could be at times. "I feel for you," I said.

"No, you don't, nigga. You love that I'm suffering right now."

"That ain't true. And there's no reason you should be suffering as long as your hands are working."

"That's easy for you to say. You ain't dating Rosy Palm every night no more," she replied, scowling.

"All I'm saying is some release is better than none at all."

"Will you help me?' she asked shyly.

"Help you how?"

"It's hard to concentrate long enough for me to get there by myself, but maybe… maybe with you here I can."

"Not with my brother and sister in the other room, you can't," I said emphatically.

"Kendrick and Keisha had a sleepover at one of their classmate's house for a birthday party. That's where your mom was going."

"Oh. Well, how long will they be gone?"

"At least another half an hour because your mom promised them McDonald's for breakfast."

Part of me knew I was gonna regret my decision, but my curiosity was getting the best of me.

"So, what do you need me to do?" I asked.

"I don't know. Just sit there, I guess."

That sounded easy enough until I saw her reach inside her pajama pants. Our eyes locked and I saw her hand moving slowly in between her legs. My first thought was she was just fucking with me. Even when her breathing became more shallow I wasn't all the way convinced. But when the scent of her pussy hit my nostrils, I knew shit was real. It took everything in me to keep from drooling down the front of my shirt.

"You're really doing it," I said in awe.

"Y-yeah," she moaned.

I considered myself a man who pays attention to a woman's body, but I'd never seen this storm that was building inside her right before my eyes. The faster her hand moved, the more interesting it got. Her face was flushed, her eyes were swimming in and out of focus, I could see little beads of sweat on her forehead, and all of it had my dick harder than a muthafucka! I had to sit back on the couch and rearrange myself to relieve some of the pressure, and that's when I had the worst idea. The rationale I worked out in my mind was as long as I didn't touch her, technically I wasn't cheating. Plus it wasn't exactly fair what she was doing to me.

Without warning I unzipped my pants, pulled my dick out, and started stroking it slowly. For a split second her eyes bulged and she completely stopped what she was doing to watch me, biting her lip in a way that just made me harder. I guess she took what I did as a challenge, because the next thing I knew she pulled her pajama pants off and sat back on the couch with her legs spread in my direction so I could see her pushing two fingers in and out of herself while a third tended to her clit. Her pussy juice was running like a waterfall down the crack of her ass and onto the couch, but we were too caught up in the moment to care. The faster I moved, the faster she moved, and we were both headed in the same direction.

"Gah. Ahmani, I'ma c-cum," she panted.

"Do it, c-cum for me."

"I'd r-rather cum o-on you," she said, moving her fingers faster.

I could hear how wet she was, and that shit was driving me crazy! It was suicide for me to have a woman, especially this particular woman, playing with herself in front of me. Who does that? Who plays with that type of fire? The moment her body bucked because it was being rocked by her orgasm, I knew what type of nigga played with fire like that: one who wanted to be burned.

"Come here," I said hungrily.

The words weren't out of my mouth good before she was in my lap, easing her hot, slippery, tight pussy down my dick slowly. Whatever I'd thought about her telling me she hadn't had sex for a while before now went out the window because she was virgin tight. With her first rise and fall I knew I'd be cumming in a matter of minutes, and when she swiveled her hips I feared it would be seconds instead of minutes. The most electrifying part was how she hovered no more than a breath away from my face and just kept constant eye contact while we fucked.

It was a battle for dominance while looking into each other's souls. I felt like I was under her spell, but too soon it was shattered by the banging on the door. We both froze like we'd been caught, but my hands on her hips were preventing her from getting up.

"Keep going," I whispered, grabbing her ass and pulling her toward me while I lifted up into her.

She opened her mouth to mine and our kisses contained our sounds of passion, but apparently we weren't being quiet enough because the banging on the door persisted.

"Ahmani! Th-the door. We gotta get th-the door."

I knew what she was trying to say, but I was too close to stop now.

"Prince William Police Department," someone shouted after the next round of banging.

This time when we froze it was only momentary because I was lifting her off me and jumping up seconds later. My first instinct was to go out the window, but Elyse must've sensed it because she grabbed my arm and shook her head.

"You haven't done anything, Ahmani. Put your dick away and answer the door," she said, pulling her pajama pants back on.

I took a deep breath and fixed myself before going to the door.

"Can I help you?" I asked, opening the door partially.

"Is this the residence of Tamika Monroe?" a tall black cop asked.

"It is, but she's not here right now."

"And you are?" he asked.

"I'm her oldest son."

"Sir, I'm gonna need you to come with me."

"What did he do, Officer?" Elyse asked, coming up behind me.

"Nothing, ma'am. We need his help."

"Help? You need my help for what?" I asked warily.

"There's been a shooting."

"I don't know nothing about that. I've been here —
"

"The shooting involves your mother."

Aryanna

Chapter Thirteen

Life in the projects came with the knowledge there would be gunplay. When disenfranchised people were put on top of those disillusioned with society's meaning of the word "equality", the end result was a bunch of individuals with one thing in common: no hope. Sure, there was light at the end of the tunnel, but it was dim and fading fast, and everyone seemed to be running out of patience. The United States has a habit of not minding its own business and always involving itself in someone else's war, but it ignores the war zones that are its own projects. Not a block away from the most powerful and famous house in the entire world, the White House, there were the projects. And dead bodies. I'd lived with the reality of what I was surrounded by and entrenched in since I was old enough to understand, and it was for this reason I prayed.

But as life so often taught us, sometimes prayers came with different answers than we wanted. As soon as the cop said the shooting involved my mom, I started praying. I wouldn't wish jail on anyone, especially not my own mother, and in truth I felt some guilt because I knew she'd been mad because of me. The cop didn't give us any details, but I knew her being mad enough to pull the trigger was a direct result of our last argument. When Elyse and I hopped into the Hummer to follow the cop, I kept praying, hoping whomever my mom had shot would survive so she wouldn't be charged with murder.

There was no way I could've known how bad I'd misread the situation. My first thought was the cop must've been new or lost because he made a right coming out of my mom's development, which only led to the Woodlawn Apartments and townhouses. That was a dead end, and he should've made the left that would've taken us deeper into the city where the police station was. Even knowing this, I still followed him, but the bad feeling I had turned worse as I saw the scene we were approaching. An ambulance passed us heading in the opposite direction, but directly in front of us were half a dozen police cars and plenty of yellow tape to keep people away.

It became quickly obvious to me the shooting had literally happened right around the corner from the house. Elyse and I looked at each other with the same *oh shit* expression, but we still don't know how bad things really were. It seemed like we spotted my mom's white Ford Taurus at the same time, parked at an angle on the curb directly in the middle of all the yellow tape and activity, but I would never remember the words we exchanged. All the neighborhood people around faded from my vision, along with the cops and medical people. The only thing I could see were all the holes in the side of my mom's car. No matter how hard I prayed, I couldn't un-see what I was looking at, nor could I deny its implications. In that instant, the officer's words came back to me about how he'd needed my help, and unless there was some type of standoff he wanted me to talk my mom down from, it was clear what he needed.

Positive identification.

I'll never know how I managed to get out of the truck and follow the cop, or how I held it together long enough for him to lift the bloody sheet and show me my mom's lifeless eyes. It was all a blur, something I refused to accept, which meant I didn't need to store it in my memory. But the aching pain with every beat of my heart argued with me on how real everything was. No one can prepare for waking up in a living nightmare anymore than they can anticipate how dark shit can really get. Seeing my beautiful mother lying there amongst broken glass, used condoms, and disregarded needles was the lowest point in my life.

Until the cop told me my brother and sister had been in the ambulance that passed us a few minutes ago, it took me a few moments to fight off the blackout my subconscious was begging for. With Elyse's help I managed to stumble to the truck, and she drove us to the hospital.

I didn't know how much time had passed since my world came to an end, or how long we'd been sitting in the E.R. waiting room. All I had the mental capacity to do was pray.

"Ahmani! Oh, my God, Ahmani," Katrina cried out, running down the hallway toward me.

I didn't even have the strength to stand up and put my arms around her, but she dropped to her knees in front of me and pulled me to her. It hadn't crossed my mind to call her because all I could think about was Kendrick and Keisha, but having her there helped. Elyse had attempted to comfort me, and even though I knew she meant well, I couldn't accept it because of what we had been doing while my mother lay dying. The guilt I felt was physically causing me pain. I'd already thrown up twice, once actually on myself, which was probably masking the smell of sex on me. I couldn't go more than a few minutes without reliving the argument my mother and I had, and every time I played it back I felt more of my sanity chip away.

"Baby, I'm so sorry. When you didn't answer your phone, I decided to go to your mom's, and that's when I found out what happened. Why, Ahmani? Why would someone do this?" Katrina asked, shaking her head.

"I don't know. Witnesses said it was a drive-by, and the cops are thinking mistaken identity."

"Maybe it was somebody sending her a message," Elyse said bitterly, looking directly at Katrina.

I would've been lying if I said that thought hadn't crossed my mind a few times since all this went down, but it seemed a little far-fetched. I knew Elyse was hurt and she was just lashing out in pain, but I didn't need the drama.

"Chill," I told her before she really had a chance to go in on Katrina.

"Why is she here, anyway?" Katrina asked, screwing her face up in obvious displeasure.

"Yo, you need to chill, too. This ain't the time or place for the bullshit, and if either of you can't respect that, then get the fuck out," I said, leaning away from Katrina so she could see the serious look on my face.

Elyse got up and walked down the hall, but I knew she wasn't headed for the door. She was just putting space between her and Katrina.

"You're right, baby. I'm sorry. I don't wanna fight with you, especially not after everything that's happened. Have you heard anything?"

"No, they're still in surgery. Kendrick took two bullets, Keisha got three."

"I'm so, so sorry, Ahmani. If there's anything I can do, just say it."

Part of me wanted to scream at her to stop coming at me with those hollow-ass platitudes that didn't mean a goddamn thing, but I knew she meant well. My guilt was definitely eating at me, but my rage was battling for that top spot. For the first time in my life I had a hunger for blood, and I wanted to kill whoever was responsible for today's destruction. I wanted them and their family! I had done a lot of dirt, but nothing that called for this to happen. The police's angle didn't seem to make sense, either. I mean, how could you mistake a woman and two kids for anything other than a woman and two kids? My mother had lived in Manassas her whole life, so there weren't a lot of muthafuckas who didn't know who she was. Why had they killed her? I needed answers, and I knew one way to get them.

"You really wanna help?" I asked Katrina.

"Yes, baby. Just tell me what you need."

"I want answers, but muthafuckas ain't gonna want to give them freely. I need to put the word out in the street that I can pay for those answers."

"I'm worth millions, but —"

"'But' what?" I asked impatiently.

"How do you know the answers you get will be the truth? When you put a price out there, every thirsty muthafucka in the city is gonna give you some type of story."

"Let me worry about that. Are you gonna put your money where your mouth is or naw?"

"Whatever you need, I got you," she replied without hesitation.

I kissed her on the forehead and stood up, pulling my phone from my pocket. I wasted no time dialing the number, knowing he was probably expecting my call.

"Yo?"

"You heard what happened?" I asked.

"Yeah. I'm sorry, bruh, but you know I'm already on top of shit," Black Boy replied,

"I want answers, bruh. Real answers, and real goddamn quick."

"I do, too. You know we family, my nigga, so I'ma do everything I gotta do. Any word on the young'ins?" he asked.

"No, not yet. Listen, I got a hundred grand for the right name, but you need to make it clear it better be the right name."

"This real money, bruh?" he asked, clearly wondering if my grief was writing a check my ass couldn't cash.

"It's legit, you got my word on that."

"I'll get back to you as soon as I know something," he replied, hanging up.

Black Boy was vicious when he wanted to be and loyal at all times, so I knew if anyone could find out who did this and why, it would be him.

"Baby, I'm not from the streets, so I won't pretend to know how these things work. I do know sometimes things happen in life that can't be explained, and that's one of the hardest things to accept. Saying how sorry I am won't change what happened, but I'm here for you, no matter what," she promised, taking my hand in hers.

I couldn't begin to describe the pain I was feeling, but I knew she could understand better than anyone. Her own tragedy was still fresh, and yet here she was trying to comfort me through mine. That took a special kind of woman, and I gave her a gentle kiss on the lips in gratitude.

"Mr. Monroe," the doctor called out, coming in our direction.

I felt an immediate tightness in my chest that made it hard to breath. The doctor was an average white guy, about two inches shorter than me with a square-shaped head that looked awkward bald. He seemed gentle and approachable, but right now I was more terrified of him than I'd ever been of anyone in my life.

"H-how are they?" I asked, hopeful.

"Mr. Monroe, w-we did everything we could. I'm so sorry."

Aryanna

Chapter Fourteen

Ten days later

Dying was a part of life, but it was still the hardest part for those left behind to mourn. Saying goodbye was never an easy or natural thing, especially if those lost to you were taken in a sudden way. With older people, you were given time to prepare, time to make lasting memories that would be held onto long after their number was called. It was still hard to lose some you loved, but at least if they were old you knew they'd lived a full life. My brother and sister never had that chance, and truthfully neither did my mother. They'd died too young, and the truth of that refused to let me grieve. I was just so angry!

It had been three days since their funeral service, and I kept waiting for some sign time would help heal the hole in my heart, but all I felt was anger. If it hadn't been for Katrina, there probably wouldn't have been a service for those I'd lost because I couldn't see past the hatred eating away at me. It was like the hatred and guilt were feeding off of each other, making every thought passing through my mind one about revenge. The only problem was I had no one to exact my revenge on.

Black Boy still had his ear to the street, and from what I'd heard he was on a warpath to get answers, taking mercy on no one. The only time he'd surfaced without his assault rifle was when he and the rest of the hood had showed out for the funeral. By now everyone knew the price I'd put out there, and I could feel the fear in the air because they knew with that type of number, nothing short of a massacre was coming. I wanted to be down in the trenches with Black Boy, but Katrina convinced me to go with her so she could take care of me.

I'd tried to go back to my mom's house only once, but I couldn't force myself to get out of the truck and go in. It wasn't just the fact I couldn't take being surrounded by memories of everything I'd lost, but Elyse was behind that door, too, and I wasn't ready to face her. I didn't blame her in any way because us having sex had been a mutual thing, but I just kept hearing the argument between my mom and me about my relationship with Katrina and me being a good dad. I thought my feelings for Katrina would've changed because of that very same argument, but she'd been so great since everything had happened that it was hard not to want to be with her. She understood when I needed silence and her presence at the same time. She also understood when I needed to be alone.

I may not have considered myself grieving in the moment, but it helped to have someone there who understood what real suffering felt like. She hadn't even judged me when I told her I needed a pound of weed and several bottles of Hennessy to be kept around at all times. She just made it happen. I managed to hold it together through the funeral, but since then I'd been in a constant fog that left me numb to all the things I didn't want to feel. Could I stay like this forever? If Katrina's money was as long as she said it was, then I'd find out.

"Baby, didn't you hear me calling you?" she asked, coming into the bedroom.

For a moment she looked like a mirage I was seeing in the cloud of smoke floating in the room, but I knew that was just the Blueberry Kush talking.

"Nah, I didn't hear you. What's up?"

"Obviously you are, but I wanted to know if you wanted something to eat."

"Nah, I'm straight," I replied, taking another pull off the blunt I was holding.

"Babe, you ain't ate in three days. You can't just live on weed and liquor."

The look I leveled at her was meant to tell her to shut it up because I didn't want any lectures, but the way she was looking at me said she was concerned. I knew I'd been more or less in the same position doing the same shit since after the funeral, but there wasn't really anything important I had to do.

"Don't nag me, Katrina."

"If I was nagging you, I'd say something about the fact you ain't showered in days," she replied, turning her nose up.

"Whatever, I don't stink," I replied defensively.

"Baby, I'm your woman, and I'd never lie to you. You stink."

"It doesn't matter if I do. Where am I going? Who am I trying to impress?"

"You're right, I just thought getting a hot shower and some food might make you feel better," she said calmly.

"You know what would make me feel better? Torturing the muthafucka who killed my mom, brother, and sister. Can you deliver that to me instead of pizza?"

"I'm working on it."

"How the fuck are you working on it?" I asked sarcastically.

"I added $400,000 more to the reward."

"Y-you what?"

"I went and saw Ira myself, and I told him the ticket was now a half a million dollars on the head of whoever killed your family," she replied matter-of-factly.

For a second I just looked at her because I didn't know what to say. I didn't know what touched me more, the money or the fact she'd actually gone to see Black Boy without me asking or suggesting it. After putting the blunt in the ashtray on the nightstand, I picked up my phone and called Black Boy.

"Hello?" a woman answered.

"Let me speak to Black Boy."

"It's Amee, Ahmani. He's right here, but I wanted to hear your voice so I'd know you're alright."

"I'm fine, Amee. How are you holding up?" I asked.

"Don't you be worrying about me right now, Ahmani, because I'm fine. I'm so sorry about what happened. You know I loved your family like my own."

"I know, sis. I love you for that," I replied, feeling that tightness in my chest again.

"I wanna see you soon. I love you. Here's Ira."

"What up, bruh?" he asked, getting on the phone.

"Maintaining. I just wanted to touch base with you and find out what's going on."

"You know I'm out here in these streets. I wanted to call and check on you, but your girl told me you were okay."

"You saw her, huh?" I asked, looking over at Katrina.

"Fucked me up when she came through here looking for me, but I respect it. She ridin' for you, bruh."

"I see that. You heard anything yet?"

"Nah, I just put the new figures on the street, but it's gonna happen, and I'ma call you as soon as it does."

"Be safe out there, and give Amee a hug for me," I said.

"We got you."

I hung up the phone feeling a different type of sadness because my mom had misjudged Katrina before she had a chance to know her. If she could see her now, she'd love her.

"Thank you, baby," I said sincerely.

"Who's Amee?"

"She's like a sister to me. We all grew up together, and she has a baby by one of my cousins."

"By your cousin, or by you?" she asked slowly.

"What's that supposed to mean?"

"I'm just asking, Ahmani. I mean, you did just say you loved her."

"Of course I love her. I've known her all my life, but that don't mean we have a baby together. We've never even had sex!"

"Okay, I'm sorry, baby. I was only wanting clarity," she said, holding her hands up in surrender as she climbed on the bed next to me.

"Don't be insecure, Katrina, please."

"I'm not insecure, sweetheart. I just don't want any secrets from the past coming up suddenly."

Her words made me think of the literal growing secret I was keeping from her, but there was no way this was the time for that conversation.

"Why you all up on me if I smell so bad?" I asked, leaning away from her.

"The Blueberry Kush covers up most of the funk. Besides, you're my man, and I love you."

"Y-you what?" I asked, wondering if I'd heard her right.

"I love you, Ahmani."

"How? We just met."

"I didn't know there was a time limit on love. I don't remember reading that fine print anywhere. I know I love you, though. Do you have a problem with that?"

Did I have a problem with that? Should I really have an issue with some rich white girl claiming to love me? Other than the fact I wasn't in love with her and I had a baby on the way with my ex, I guess I didn't see a problem. Granted, those two things were huge fucking deals!

"It's not that I have a problem with it, it's just early in our relationship. You may think you love me, but you could change your mind."

"So you doubt my love, my ability to love, or my ability to know what love is when I feel it?" she asked, crossing her arms over her chest.

The expression on her face was universal for "Choose your next words wisely." Having an in-depth philosophical conversation on love's many definitions wasn't how I planned to spend the rest of my afternoon, so I chose a different approach.

"That question is a setup if I've ever heard one, so let me better explain. What I'm saying is love is a verb requiring constant and consistent action, and we've only been together for a little while."

"Oh, so you want me to prove my love. Why didn't you just say that?" she asked, pulling the covers back to reveal my naked body.

Before I knew it her panties hit the floor, and she was astride me with her hand beneath her t-shirt and in between her legs, taking hold of my dick and guiding it inside her. My protests were made in vain because I knew she was tired of being denied, especially since we hadn't had sex since that day at my apartment. Honestly, pussy had been the last thing on my mind because I couldn't think about it without Elyse being in the equation.

I definitely wasn't seeing her now, though. Katrina had my undivided attention as she rode me fast and hard, cumming twice within the first five minutes, but never breaking stride. When I attempted to roll her beneath me, I found out how strong she was because she pinned me to the bed, her hands on my chest and her nails digging in.

Even when I started bucking beneath her, trying to drill my dick up through her lungs, she wouldn't relinquish control. She rode me like a wild stallion, cumming so hard I thought she might go into shock. It wasn't until I was about to get mine that she hopped off me and told me if I wanted it, I had to come get it. I knew I was being led by my dick, but I followed her into the shower anyway and made her climb the walls while she screamed out how much she loved me. I couldn't deny I needed what she was giving me, which was a constructive way to release the chaos of emotions I was carrying inside.

After our first round in the shower, she left me in there to wash up, but soon came back with her late father's stash of little blue pills.

"Do you know what you're getting yourself into?" I asked her.

"We need this, baby. We're all we got."

With the swallowing of the first pill, the battle was on. For the next eight hours we ran a marathon of fucking, and I got to see how much of a freak Katrina was. There was nothing off limits, and I damn sure put that to the test, because I put her in every position I could think of. I fucked her in her ass until it bled. I beat the pussy up until it went dry and the lips swelled up like airbags. I lost track of how much of my cum she swallowed, but she sucked dick like it was the only way to get into the gates of heaven!

At one point during our second or third trip to one of the many showers in the house, I told her to stand there while I pissed on her. Not only did she do it, but as soon as I was done she popped the dick right back in her mouth and sucked it until my knees gave out! I'd never in my life met anyone like her, and by 11:00 p.m. that night I knew I'd be a fucking fool to go looking.

"Have I proven a part of my love for you?" she asked, passing me the blunt she'd just fired up as we lay in bed together.

"You did, but damn, I had no idea you got down like that."

"Trust me, that's not the norm. I ain't never let a man just have his way with me, especially not how you were doing."

"Yeah, right," I replied, inhaling the Kush hard.

"I swear to you on the lives of my parents, baby. I ain't never let a muthafucka fuck me in the ass like that, piss on me, or pull my hair out at the roots."

"I'm sorry about that. The head was too damn good and I lost control for a second."

"It's fine, baby, but what I'm saying is the things you and I did today I only did because I love you, because I trust you, and because we both needed it," she said, cuddling up next to me.

"I did need that. I'm sorry if I hurt you, though."

"You didn't. I needed it, too, because I have a lot built up I can't express with words. It's not just the loss, but the guilt, too. Why them and not me? My parents shouldn't have died at the hands of a muthafucka who was obsesses with me."

I put my arm around her and pulled her close, not needing to give a voice to my own guilt because I knew she got it. I felt lucky to have someone who understood by my side to go through this with me, because I didn't know if I could survive being alone in that moment.

"We'll get through this together," I said, passing the blunt back to her.

"I agree, but we have to be willing to do what's necessary."

"What do you mean?"

"I wanna show you something," she replied, getting out of bed and motioning for me to follow her.

She led me downstairs, through the living room, and came to a stop at a door next to her father's office. She hesitated for a second and looked at me, but then she turned the knob and stepped through the doorway. I followed her down a flight of stairs into a dimly-lit basement, my nose tingling with a familiar smell in the air that I couldn't quite place.

"What is this?" I asked once we got to the bottom.

"The range."

She hit some switches on the wall and row after row of lights began to flicker on, revealing a basement that had been converted into a home gun range.

"Were you stockpiling for a war?" I asked, looking at all the different kinds of guns lining the wall directly opposite the bottom of the stairs.

"My dad said it was better to be safe than sorry."

"That's one way to look at it. Was your dad one of those end-of-the-world, doomsday people?"

"Not at all, he simply believed if you stayed ready, you didn't have to get ready."

"Okay, so what are we doing down here, exactly?" I asked.

"It's time you learned how to handle a gun. It's time you choose which direction your life goes from here."

"What do you mean?"

"You gotta decide. Are you a predator, or the prey?"

Chapter Fifteen

Three days later

It surprised the shit out of me how good Katrina was with a gun, but it was hella sexy watching her work. I'd been around plenty of shooters, enough to know the professional from the amateur, and Katrina was professional. She taught me what she knew, and I had to admit the type of power I felt when I pulled the trigger was unlike anything I'd ever experienced. It kept me higher than any blunt I smoked, and surprisingly it was more stress-relieving than fucking the life out of Katrina.

After that first night, I spent more and more time in the basement, wanting the Glock .45 Katrina had given me to feel like a second skin. The more bullets I fired into the targets set up at the end of the basement, the more convinced I became that I had to be the one to drop the hammer on whoever killed my people. Once upon a time I didn't think I was about that life. Times had changed.

"You been down there all night?" Katrina asked when I walked into the kitchen.

Before I answered, I took the time to admire her beautiful nakedness. Whenever we were in the house, she insisted she had to be in the nude just in case I wanted a quickie. She tried to make it seem like this was for my benefit and her concession of the dutiful girlfriend, but really I knew she was hoping to entice me because she wanted the dick.

"I went down about 2:00 a.m. I couldn't sleep."

"Really? I thought I put it on you good, but I guess I gotta work harder," she said, setting a plate of waffles, eggs, and bacon in front of me.

"Trust me, baby, you do what you do very well. I just had a bad dream and couldn't sleep."

I knew I wouldn't have to elaborate because there had been a few nights when I held her after she had sleep snatched from her by a nightmare. She'd done the same for me, too. It still wasn't easy dealing with everything that had happened, but we were there for each other, and that made shit bearable.

"Why do you have shorts on?" she asked, sitting on my lap.

"Because I can't concentrate when I'm shooting naked. Too much dick moving around. I worry a hot shell is gonna do some irreversible damage."

"We definitely can't have that," she said, sticking her hand into my shorts and lightly massaging the topic of conversation.

"Are you gonna let me eat, babe?"

"I guess, although I wish you were eating me."

"Last time I did that you almost lost your voice and your mind," I replied, laughing.

"You're an asshole for bringing that up, and I had no idea it could be that good," she said, hitting me in the chest and laughing with me.

"I warned you, didn't I? You thought I was bullshittin'."

"I kinda did, but when you started off by biting me and sending that shockwave through my body, I knew there was trouble. When you licked my asshole, that was some next-level shit, and I was lost."

"You're welcome. Now feed me my breakfast and I might take you to the moon before I go."

"Where you going?" she asked casually, pouring syrup on my apple cinnamon waffles.

"I'm going to Manassas."

I was waiting on her next question, but she just went about cutting up my waffles and started feeding me. The first time she'd cooked for me I'd been as surprised as she had been when I'd done it for her, but I gave her credit for her skills. Us playing house seemed to work out better than I'd thought it would.

"When I got up this morning, I had a message on my phone. Aaron is awake, and he's gonna be arraigned next week."

"You don't sound happy about that," I replied, chewing slowly.

"I'm not happy about it. I don't want him going to court. I want him in the fucking ground."

Her tone of voice caused me to bite my tongue on accident. The coldness was a surprise because I'd never heard that from her before, but I could understand it.

The look in her eyes as she continued feeding me said she was thinking something she wasn't saying.

"What?" I asked.

"I didn't say anything, baby."

"I know you didn't, but I can see you've got something to say, so spit it out."

Still she hesitated until I took the fork full of eggs from her hand and sat it back on the plate.

"I want him dead, Ahmani."

"And?"

"And I want you to help me."

"How?"

"I figured I could pay your brother to…."

She let the words trail off, but we both knew what she wanted Black Boy to do. We both also knew what wasn't being said when it came to how much she was helping me settle the score for what had happened with my family. I knew Katrina would never come out of her mouth and say I owed her, but I did owe her.

"I'll talk to him."

"Can I – can I come with you?" she asked softly.

I wanted to say no because we hadn't had any time apart. The look in her eyes said she didn't wanna be alone, though.

"We've gotta get going, so you should probably go get dressed," I told her.

She grabbed my face and kissed me like my lungs contained the last bit of oxygen in the world, and she was determined to get to it. I don't know when her hand got back into my shorts, but I had to stop her before we didn't make it out of the house.

"Don't start, babe. I just told you we gotta go."

"I was only gonna give it a little kiss," she replied with a teasing smile.

"Yeah, right. You can do that later," I said, pushing her off my lap and smacking her on the ass so she would go.

It was hard fighting temptation, because the way her ass shook had me wanting to do a few things. Luckily for the both of us she did like I told her, and I went back to eating my breakfast. Once I was done, I made my way upstairs and got me something to wear while I waited on her to finish up in the shower. I would've got in with her, but that was a counterproductive move.

I'd just finished up my text to Black Boy when she came out of the shower with a look in her eyes that spelled trouble.

"Baby, do you like when my pussy is completely shaved, or do you like a little landing strip?"

Naturally this question drew my attention to the sweet spot in between her legs, which was her intention.

"Behave, woman," I said, pinching her nipple as I walked past.

"You love it when I'm naughty."

"I do," I replied, laughing.

"See, I knew you loved me."

Her words stopped me in my tracks as I gave them careful consideration. Did I love her? Part of love was trust, honesty, and understanding, and we had all of that. I couldn't see loving someone without loyalty being involved, and we had that too. So far as I could tell I was the only one keeping a major secret, but even God kept secrets, and that didn't mean He didn't love us. So what was missing? Turning around to look at her standing there, I couldn't think of any one thing that was missing.

"You're right. I do love you."

"Y-you what?" she whispered, her hand going to her mouth.

"I love you, Katrina."

She took two steps and jumped, and I caught her, holding her close as she clung to me. I could feel her body shaking, but I didn't know if she was cold or crying.

"Baby, it's okay," I said, rubbing her back.

"I love you so much, Ahmani, and I've been so afraid to tell you how much because I thought you didn't love me back."

After the conversation we'd had a few days ago that led to the greatest sexual experiences of my life, we hadn't talked about love again, so I could understand her fear.

"I should've told you sooner, baby. I do love you, though."

I could feel her tears on my face as she kissed me all over, and I could taste the saltiness when our lips connected.

"Don't cry. It's okay. I'll tell you over and over again, I promise. Right now, I need to take a shower, though."

"Take me with you," she said, refusing to unlock her legs or arms from around me.

I quit putting up a fight and carried her to the shower with me. Just as I'd feared, it was over an hour later before we resurfaced.

"Don't you smile at me. Now I gotta text my brother and tell him we're running late," I said, drying off while she did the same with a satisfied, shit-eating grin on her face.

"It's not my fault," she replied innocently.

I threw my towel at her and grabbed my boxers. She disappeared into the closet to get dressed, and I quickly put on my white button-up, Black Billionaire jeans, and my black Jordans.

"I'll meet you in the truck," I hollered, grabbing my phone and going downstairs. I didn't stop at the first floor, though. I went to the basement and grabbed my Glock, making sure it was fully loaded before tucking it in my jeans. I got back upstairs and into the kitchen just as she was walking out into the garage.

"Love the outfit," I said, admiring her ass in the black yoga pants she had on.

When she turned around, my eyes immediately went to her hard nipples beneath the white wife-beater she was wearing.

"Thanks. My shoes match, huh?" she asked, looking down at the black and white Chuck Taylors on her feet.

She knew damn well I wasn't looking at her shoes. "Funny," I said, reaching for the keys to the truck.

"I'm driving, baby," she informed me, grabbing the key to the Porsche. I started to object, but in truth I had been wanting to go for a ride in that bad muthafucka.

"You might wanna put your seatbelt on," she said once we were in the car.

I did a she suggested, respecting the growl of the engine when she cranked it. She backed out slowly, but once we cleared the driveway there was smoke everywhere from her standing on the gas pedal. I was thrown deep in the seat, and that's where I stayed for the entire ride to Manassas. It should've taken us an hour, but we were rolling through Georgetown South in thirty minutes, easily. I texted Black Boy and told him we were there just as we pulled up next to his car.

"Stay here," I said, stepping out once he came out of his house.

"What's up, bruh?"

"It's good to see you," he replied, giving me a hug.

"I'm a'ight. Any word yet?"

"Nothing that's made sense or turned into anything, but you know I got every nigga I know shaking the city like we looking for lunch money."

"What's not making sense?" I asked.

"I don't think no nigga from around here pulled the trigger. I mean, for the type of bread you putting up, a muthafucka's momma would put his name in the street. So, if it's an out-of-town shooter, then that means he was paid to do a job, and I just can't see nobody coming at your mom like that."

A hitman after my mom? I couldn't even imagine a situation where my mom would put herself in that kind of trouble.

"Hey, you," Amee said, coming out of her house and walking slowly toward us.

"What's up, light skin?" I asked pulling her into a bear hug and kissing the top of her head.

"You look good. You know I've been worried about you," she said, looking up at me.

"I know, but I'm holding up as best as I can."

"Why do you have a gun on you?" she asked, not taking her arms from around my waist.

"Just being prepared for whatever."

"When did you start carrying a pistol, bruh? You don't even know how to shoot," Black Boy said.

"I taught him."

I wasn't sure when Katrina had gotten out of the car, but there she was, standing with the door open, looking at Amee with hate in her eyes.

"Come here, baby," I said, introducing them, but making sure to keep them an arm's length apart. Amee may have been in constant pain because of her RSD, but she knew how to inflict pain, too, and was not above twisting a bitch's wig.

"Hey," Amee said.

"Hey."

"So, you taught him how to shoot?" Black Boy asked skeptically.

"Yeah. I learned when I was about twelve years old."

"Yo, she ain't no joke," I said, vouching for her. The look Black Boy gave me was one of clear disbelief, but I kept shaking my head.

"Where did you learn to shoot?" he asked her.

"In my basement."

"That shit is a legit gun range, my nigga, no lie," I told him.

"Y'all gonna have to invite a nigga over for dinner or something so I can see this for myself," Black Boy said.

"So, you two are living together, Ah—"

"I actually got a business proposition for you," Katrina said, turning to Black Boy after cutting Amee off.

The look Amee gave me telegraphed what she wanted to do, but I put my hands up in a placating gesture, trying to get her to chill.

"What's the proposition?" Black Boy asked.

Katrina didn't immediately respond. She looked at Amee, and then back to Black Boy.

"You can speak in front of her. She's family," I said.

"Okay. Well, the muthafucka who killed my parents is awake in the hospital now, and they said he'll be arraigned next week."

"And you don't want that to happen," Back Boy said, nodding his head in understanding.

"How much?" Katrina asked.

"Since it's short notice, it's gonna be $50,000."

"We'll be back in about a half an hour," she said.

"We will?" I asked.

"Yes, baby. We just gotta go to my house because the banks are closed by now."

"A'ight, we'll be back, bruh. Bye Amee," I said giving her a quick hug. She hugged me back, but she kept her eyes on Katrina.

"You drive," Katrina said, going around to the passenger side.

"Don't wreck that muthafucka, bruh. You'd have to hit a lot of houses to pay for it," Black Boy said, laughing.

"No, he wouldn't. It's his car," Katrina said.

"Since when?" I asked, dumbfounded.

"Since now. I just gave it to you," she replied, smiling.

"Damn, it's like that? You got a sister?" Black Boy asked seriously.

I was still laughing as I climbed behind the wheel and adjusted everything for its new owner. Me. "Are you really giving me this car, babe?"

"Why are you so surprised? We can go buy a new one if you want."

"Nah, this one right here is good to go."

I was just about to back up when my phone started ringing. I pulled it out and answered it without paying attention to who was calling.

"Yo?"

"We need to talk. Can you meet me?" Elyse asked.

"Nah, I'm doing something right now."

"It's important. The DNA results are in."

Chapter Sixteen

It took some fast-talking to get Katrina to take the car and go to her house after dropping me at my mom's, but there was no scenario where her seeing Elyse went well. I hadn't told her Elyse had been staying at my mom's since everything had happened, and right then that omission was working to my advantage. I really didn't want to be there, but knowing for sure if I was gonna be a father made it necessary. I took a deep breath, hoping the shaking in my hands would stop as I knocked on the door.

"Hey, stranger," Elyse said, opening the door wider so I could come in. I don't know how my legs were moving, but before I knew it I was standing in the living room.

A million thoughts came rushing at me about the last time I'd seen my mom here, and the promise I'd made to take Keisha and Kendrick to Chuck E. Cheese. Memories of their voices echoing off the walls filled my ears. When I looked at the couch, I saw Elyse on top of me, scratching an itch only I could satisfy. I felt overwhelmed by all the emotions running through me, but there was no way to avoid them as long as I was in this house.

"How have you been?" Elyse asked, coming up behind me.

"That's a dumb question."

"You're right, I'm sorry. I've spent most of my nights crying, so I can only imagine how hard all this has been on you. I miss them so much. They were more my family than the one I was born into."

I opened my mouth to say some slick shit, but I didn't because the love she had for my mom and siblings was real. I knew that.

"How have you been?" I asked.

"That's a dumb question," she replied, smiling through the tears.

I pulled her into my arms and hugged her, and for the first time I cried. Maybe it was being back in the house, or maybe it was knowing Elyse could feel my pain because we'd lost the same people. The reason didn't matter. We just held on to each other and cried. It seems like the tears would never stop, but I somehow managed to get myself under control.

"I can't believe I cried in front of you," I said.

"I can. I know damn well you ain't crying in front of your new girlfriend."

"It's not because she wouldn't understand, because she would. It's just that —"

"You don't owe me any explanations, Ahmani. If you're happy, then I'm happy for you," she said, backing out of my embrace and picking up an envelope off the coffee table.

"I know we agreed to have the DNA test done after the baby was born, but I didn't want you to have to wait that long. I used the hair I accidentally pulled out while we were having sex as the comparison sample," she said, handing me the envelope.

I knew this was what I asked for, but now that I had the truth in my hands, I was more nervous than ever. Up until that moment I could accept or deny the child Elyse was carrying, but after I opened the results, there was no going back.

"You want me to open it?" she asked after I simply continued to look at the envelope.

"I got it," I said, finally tearing it open.

I quickly scanned the single sheet of paper inside, and then I went over it again, word for word. When I looked from the paper to Elyse, I didn't find the expression on her face I'd been anticipating. I'd expected her to be just as nervous as I was, but she was utterly calm.

"It. It says. I'm. I'm not–not sure I'm reading it right."

"You are reading it right. Just calm down and take a deep breath."

"How? How am I gonna be a father? Elyse, I don't know how to be a father," I said, feeling the beginnings of panic coming over me.

"I'm not sure how to be a mother, but we can figure this out together, for our baby's sake. We have to give him or her better than we had. As long as we keep that focus, we'll be fine."

She made it sound easy, but I knew it would never be that easy. I understood the world in ways my child was blissfully ignorant to, which meant it was my job to protect and worry about him or her. In that moment I finally understood why my mom had been the way she'd been ever since I got out. My child wasn't even in this world yet, but I could already imagine the sheer terror I would feel if he or she found him- or herself in jail, looking at life in prison. The bottom line was that no parent wanted to lose a child for any reason, and I understood that now.

Closing the distance between Elyse and I, I put my hand underneath her t-shirt and held it to her stomach, imagining our baby safe and happy.

"How far along are you?" I asked.

"The doctor says I'm sixteen weeks, and the baby is perfectly healthy."

"Can they tell what it is yet?"

"I didn't ask or wanna know until you were there with me. Will you go to my next checkup?"

"Of course I will. I'm always gonna be here for the both of you," I promised, gently rubbing her stomach.

I could see the tears of happiness in her eyes, and just the slightest hint of relief too. "Okay. So if it's a boy, I wanna name him after you. And if it's a girl, I wanna name her after your mom, if that's alright with you."

"That sounds perfect," I replied, fighting the lump in my throat. My mom had been looking forward to being a grandmother, and that opportunity had been stolen from her. The only way to make up for that was for me to be the father my mom knew I could be.

"When do we need to start shopping for the baby?" I asked.

"We've got time, but —"

My ringing phone interrupted our conversation, and I couldn't ignore it because it was Katrina.

"Hey, baby."

"Hey, I'll be out front in ten minutes. Do you want me to come in while you finish up whatever you're doing?" she asked.

"Nah, I just wanted to spend a few minutes in here. I'll meet you out front."

"Okay, I'm on my way. I love you."

"I love you, too," I replied, hanging up.

I put my phone back in my pocket, and I desperately wanted to put my hand back on Elyse's stomach, but I could feel the enormous gap between us, despite the inches of separation.

"You love her?" she asked softly.

I wanted to look her in her eyes and give her a confident response, but my eyes stayed fixed on the paper still clutched in my grasp. Complicated didn't begin to describe what this situation was or would be, and I wasn't sure how to fix it.

"Yeah, I do," I replied.

"You don't sound so sure about that, Ahmani. I don't care what lies you tell her, but don't lie to me or yourself."

"I'm not lying. I love her."

"Really? Two weeks ago we were fucking right here on this couch. Did you love her then? Look at me!" she said, grabbing my face roughly. "You don't love that bitch. You don't even know that bitch! I know Black Boy told you about what he heard when he checked her out, and I heard some of the same shit when I asked questions. Katrina ain't straight, Ahmani."

"You would say that," I replied, pulling away from her. "And I do know her. I know everything I need to know about her. You act like all we do is fuck."

"I ain't clocking how much you run dick through that cum-dumpster. That's your decision. But don't confuse above-average pussy with love, because you're smarter than that."

"You're right, I am. And trust me, I would never fall in love with above-average pussy. Besides, her pussy is a-maz-ing," I said with a smile.

My comment struck a nerve, and I could see the anger clear in her eyes. I couldn't take pleasure in it, though.

"Look, I don't wanna fight with you, and I don't want you getting upset while my baby is in there. Katrina ain't your concern, so let's just focus on bringing a healthy baby into the world, okay?"

"You can tell yourself she ain't my problem, but if you plan on having my baby around her, then she is. You can act like you don't know that for the next five months if it makes you feel better, but it won't change shit. You need to start thinking straight, Ahmani, and remember what your mom said. While you're at it, you should try asking yourself if you really love Katrina, or if you love what she does for you."

This time it was her words that struck a nerve. Dropping the letter of paternity at her feet, I turned around and left. She had no right to question any emotion I felt for Katrina, especially considering the way she'd played with my heart. It was jealousy, pure and simple, and I didn't have time for that. Thankfully Katrina was pulling up as I made it to the curb.

"Move over, I'm driving," I said, opening the driver's side door and getting in.

I didn't even wait on her to put her seatbelt on before I jumped on the gas and had the car moving sideways as the tires spun. We rode in silence while I lived out my NASCAR fantasies by racing through the city, almost losing control a few times.

"You wanna talk about it?" Katrina asked.

"Talk about what?"

"Whatever is bothering you, because it's obvious you're in a different mood than when I left you. Baby, I would've stayed if I had known it would be that hard for you to go back into your mom's house. You don't have to suffer alone."

"I'm fine," I said, sliding through a left turn and still choosing to hit the gas instead of the brake.

In that moment, the smell of the rubber I was leaving behind us was as exhilarating as he gun smoke when I was blowing off steam in the basement. It was sweet Katrina wanted me to lean on her, but she was clueless as to what was really going on in my mind at the moment, and I still had no idea how I was gonna tell her the biggest part.

"Where's the money?" I asked, pulling up in front of Black Boy's car and hitting my horn.

"Right here," she replied, holding up a brown paper bag.

When Black Boy appeared from around a corner a couple minutes later, I motioned for him to go to her side of the car, but he came directly to me.

"We got a problem," he said.

"What?"

"Dude ain't in the hospital no more. He's already been moved to the jail, and they got him in segregation."

"That was fast, but why is he in the hole?" I asked.

"For the same reason they moved him out of the hospital: they're worried he'll buy his freedom if they don't get him caged in."

"Smart thinking. I doubt he goes for it, though, and at the very least his lawyer will get him put on the max security floor where I was."

"I don't want him on the max security floor. I want him dead," Katrina said through gritted teeth.

When I looked over at her, I saw she was bright red in the face and her eyes were blue ice.

"Calm down, sweetheart. He can't hide forever. As soon as he's out, we'll get it done," I assured her.

"I want it done A.S.A.P., Ahmani. A.S.A.P.! Here, it's already paid for," she said, handing me the paper bag, which I slid out the window.

Black Boy looked inside and then back at her, nodding his head.

"Consider it handled. I'll call you later, bruh," he said to me before he backed away from the car and disappeared the way he came.

"You okay?" I asked, looking at her and noticing she wasn't quite as red, but she was still a long way from calm.

"I just want it over with. Is that too much to ask?"

"Absolutely not, babe. Let's do something to take our minds off all the sadness and anger," I suggested.

"Like what?"

"I don't know, how about we —"

My phone started ringing, as it always seemed to do at the wrong time, but I still dug in my pocket to get it. This time I did look at the number, and I saw it was Elyse. I hit the ignore button.

"Who was that?"

"No one who is gonna interrupt our day together. I just wanna spend some time with you outside of the house, uninterrupted."

"Mm, I like the sound of that," she replied, leaning over and kissing me in a soft and sensual way.

My phone started ringing again, but I hit the ignore button without even looking at the screen this time. Knowing Elyse, she was probably getting ready to offer up some lame-ass apology, and I wasn't interested in all that.

"You know what I wanna do, baby?" she asked, smiling mischievously.

"After what we've done, it probably won't surprise me with your nasty ass."

"Very funny, but I'm not talking about sex. Well, not just sex. I'm thinking we should charter a jet and fly to Vegas for a couple days."

"Vegas? What are we gonna do in Vegas when we can't drink?" I asked.

"Is that really what you're worried about, Ahmani? Boy, please. When you've got money, you can do anything in Las Vegas. We can drink, do some gambling, get married, take in some shows, or —"

"Back up, back up. You talking fast, but I ain't listening slow. Say that again."

I knew I heard her perfectly the first time, and part of me had known this was the route she was headed down, which was why I'd come up with the lame excuse about being allowed to drink. It was natural progression for any woman that first come love, then comes marriage. They'd been hearing that shit since nursery school rhymes! And since Katrina moved on a faster clock, as soon as I heard the word Vegas I smelled a rat.

"I said we could drink, gamble, get married, take in a-."

"Get married? You think we're ready for that type of major move?"

"I am. I really love you, Ahmani and I —"

"Ahmani!"

I looked past Katrina at the sound of my name being called, seeing Amee coming toward us faster than I'd seen her move in years. It was obvious something was wrong.

"You didn't – you didn't answer your phone," she said, struggling to catch her breath.

"What's wrong, Amee?" I asked, starting to open my door.

"Don't get out! You gotta go. Go to the hospital. Elyse is on her way to the hospital."

Right then and there I knew real fear. I had no idea why she was going to the hospital, but there was no good reason for it. I slammed the car into first gear and stood on the gas with all my weight, cranking the wheel until the car had done a complete one-eighty and launched itself like a rocket. I tried to think, but the fear was too overwhelming, and it only allowed two words to cycle through my brain.

Get there.

"Are we seriously rushing to the hospital to your ex right now?"

"Don't start, Katrina," I warned, blowing through a stop sign and just barely missing another car.

"Don't start? What type of shit is this? I mean, you act like you still fucking that bitch or something! You're my man. That bitch needs to call her own goddamn —"

"Shut the fuck up!" I yelled, trying my hardest not to backhand the spit out of her mouth.

I wasn't one to put my hands on a female, but if she didn't let me concentrate on driving the car, I was gonna swell her tongue up so she couldn't say shit. Thankfully she didn't utter another word, even though I could feel her looking at me hard enough to set the grease in my hair on fire. Her ass was just gonna have to get over it.

The Porsche screamed to a stop and I hopped out at a dead run.

"I'm looking for Elyse Richards," I said to the first nurse I came to. She was already shaking her head, but I didn't wait for the words before I moved on.

"I'm looking for Elyse Richards," I said again, this time stopping at the nurses' station.

"Okay. She's in exam room four, which is —"

I was already on the move without her directions, fighting against the panic that was vibrating my body. I'd already lost too much. I couldn't lose my baby, too.

"Elyse!" I yelled, coming through the door and running to her bedside.

"I called you," she said.

"I'm sorry. I'm so sorry. Are you okay? Is–is the baby okay?"

"I was so scared, Ahmani. After you left I went to the bathroom, and I saw. I saw blood. He's okay, though. The doctor said occasional spotting is normal, but it terrified me."

"He? We're having a boy?"

"Yeah, you're gonna have a junior," she said, smiling through the tears.

"Wow, I —"

"Tell me she's lying, Ahmani. Tell me you didn't get that bitch pregnant."

Aryanna

Chapter Seventeen

Four months later

The sound of her breathing as she slept next to me was soothing in its own way. Her nightmares as of late had been more frequent, so any time she spent sleeping peacefully was a comfort for both of us. My only wish was that I could peek inside her mind and see what was going on in there.

After we had somehow managed to deal with the devastation of Elyse being pregnant, we'd sworn to keep no secrets between us, but Katrina guarded her nightmares with closed lips. My wanting to know what they were about was part curiosity, but mainly it was me wanting to help her if I could.

I'd had my doubts about our relationship's survival once she'd found out my truth. However, she'd surprised me by understanding my child's creation happened before me and her got together. I knew that wasn't easy to swallow, and I had more respect for her now than I ever did. I had more love for her, too. Her words of acceptance had come with actions to back them up, because there wasn't a doctor's appointment or shopping trip she hadn't been a part of. She even had one of the bedrooms in the house turned into a nursery. Her showing love for my unborn son made it hard not to love her that much more, and now I knew my feelings weren't about what she could do for me, but the incredible woman she was.

With every breath she took, even while she slept, I felt lucky to have her. The sun was just coming up outside our window, providing enough light for me to look at the platinum and diamond-encrusted wedding band on my ring finger. It felt strange to be married because it hadn't been something I envisioned this early in my life, but I had no regrets. Plus, I wanted to show Katrina she was important to me and someone I wanted in my life forever.

We didn't bring up our past relationships, but I knew her insecurities came from muthafuckas doing her wrong. I wasn't gonna add my name to that list. She may have come from money, but she hadn't had a nigga treat her like royalty until I came along. And she was gonna make a great mother someday, once I knocked her up. We'd been working on that damn-near around the clock for months, and it was still as much fun as it had been that first night. I was tempted to start something now because she looked so beautiful naked in the early morning light, but I knew how much she needed her rest. Slowly I slid from the bed, careful not to wake her, and I went to the closet to throw on my workout gear.

Once I was dressed, I grabbed my phone and headed downstairs to the gym. I'd had to get into a routine in order to keep up with Katrina's ass, because just when I thought we had reached our sexual peak, she took shit to the next level. No way was I gonna be outdone!

I was just getting ready to do my thang on the treadmill when my phone started vibrating in my hand. I recognized the number, but I was surprised he was hitting me up this early.

"Damn, did you skip breakfast to hop on the phone?" I asked, answering the call.

"I got my tray in my hand, smartass. What's up, young nigga?"

"I'm maintaining, pops. How you?"

"Living. I ain't seen you in a couple months. When you coming back up here to see me?"

"I. Don't. Know," I replied slowly, my antenna automatically going up because it was obvious he was trying to tell me something.

"I was just asking because I miss your ass. A lot."

I'd known old man Doug for a while, and the last statement he made was definitely something out of the ordinary.

"I miss you, too, pops. And you know, it's crazy that you mention seeing you, because I actually have some business out that way in a little while."

"I'll look for you," he replied, hanging up before I could say anything else.

Yeah, it was definitely some shit going on. Working out was a thing of the past, so I went back upstairs and changed into some denim polo jeans, a white t-shirt, and my butter Timbs. Katrina was still asleep, and I intended to leave her that way, but I did take the time to scribble out a note so she'd know where I was headed.

With that done, I made sure I had my I.D, phone, and some cash, and I went back downstairs. The Maybach Coupe had been my wedding present, and that's what I chose to drive.

Contrary to my initial thoughts, it hadn't been hard to get used to living life with money, and I found out how little money meant to Katrina because she insisted I didn't sign a Prenup. I'd felt weird about that, but I knew I was marrying her for love, not money.

I got on the road and only stopped long enough to grab something to eat from Hardee's, and I managed to get to the jail by 8:00 a.m. for the first round of visits. Truthfully, I hated to be anywhere near this raggedy muthafucka, but old man Doug was my dude, and I was loyal if nothing else. He was a man of his word, too, because he was one of the first people through the door for visitation.

Our visits were non-contact, and we were separated by thick-ass Plexiglas with only a phone receiver to communicate through. The jail officials could be listening in, but it was better to have a conversation this way than on the phone where we knew they were listening.

"What's up, pops?" I said once he'd picked up on his side.

"I'm okay. I appreciate you getting down here so quick."

"You know I got you, plus you sounded weird on the phone."

"I know, but I knew you were smart enough to know when something ain't right."

"Well, don't keep me in suspense, nigga. What is it?" I asked.

"You know I got your back, and I'm your eyes in here. Ol' boy finally made it out of the hole and up to the penthouse with us, and we had a conversation."

"Okay, and?"

"And he said he didn't do it. Now, before you say anything, I know that's the same line every muthafucka kicks, but I wanna tell you what he told me."

I was only halfway listening by this point because I knew whatever story the dude concocted was some bullshit. I was there, though, so I'd give old man Doug his twenty minutes of say.

"I'm listening, pops."

"A'ight. He admitted to being at your wife's house that night, but only to break up with her. He'd been trying to end it for months, but she did anything she could to manipulate him into staying. I'm talking bribery, blackmail, threatening to kill herself, anything she could think of, including faking a pregnancy. He'd stayed for a while, but eventually he had to go because the jealousy and insecurity was smothering him. That night he was only at her house because she begged him to come and said it was the last time she would bother him."

"What did you expect him to say, my nigga? He's looking at getting that heart-stopper. I know you ain't in here falling for shit like that," I said, not believing he'd actually had me come all the way down there for this.

"I been around a long time, young nigga, and I consider myself to be a good judge of character. Furthermore, I know when a nigga is kickin' shit while saying it's sugar. Even if I didn't believe the words coming out of his mouth, the fact his lawyer has pages and pages of texts from your girl speaks for itself."

This statement did get my attention. Now we were talking about proof versus suspicion.

"What do the texts say?"

"From what he's saying, it should be enough for reasonable doubt, because he insists he never saw her parents, so as far as he knows they were alive when he left. One thing he's certain about is the texts and Facebook messages he saved definitely show your lady is a little off."

I was hearing what he was saying, but none of it was adding up to the woman I knew and loved. Sure, she had some insecurity issues and she could be jealous, but nothing that fit the picture he was trying to paint.

"I hear you, but that ain't the woman I know, and I gotta stand by mine. Tell li'l buddy good luck at trial, but either way it ain't gonna make a difference. Feel me?"

"Yeah, he said you probably wouldn't hear him, but he still wanted me to warn you."

"Warn me about what?" I asked, becoming bored with the whole conversation.

"That she wouldn't be satisfied until there was nobody in your world more important than her. And if you wanted proof of that, you should holla at Robert Cook."

"Who is he?"

Old man Doug brought his hand up slowly and extended his index while holding his thumb straight up, simulating a gun, and jerked his hand in a shooting motion. After that he hung the phone up, nodded his head at me, and disappeared back into the hell he was forced to call home.

The whole way back to my car I replayed our conversation, trying to dismiss the nonsense and focus on what was real. Every time I tried to use logic and give Aaron Charles the benefit of the doubt, I couldn't because he was describing a woman who was the complete opposite of my wife. For those two people to be one and the same meant she'd have to be certifiably nuts, and no one could hide that amount of crazy for as long as she had. I knew Katrina, that much I was sure of. So why did I have such a bad feeling?

As soon as I got in the car, I grabbed my phone and called Black Boy.

"You up early, bruh. What's wrong?" he asked once he answered.

"Where you at?"

"I'm at home. Why?"

"I'll be there in fifteen minutes," I replied, hanging up and starting the car.

I knew a pair of lips would say anything, so all the bullshit this dude was peddling should've been easy to ignore, but for some reason it wasn't. There was one question I'd been asking myself since the night I'd gotten out and Katrina had told me what happened: how had I not run into the dude in that house? It was possible we had simply missed each other, but based on the cops' response time, that window was maybe two to three minutes wide.

The story had always been that some neighbor called the cops anonymously because they saw what looked like a burglar, but how the hell had they missed seeing Aaron Charles? We weren't built the same, so a one-size-fits-all explanation didn't add up. So was he really there? To ask that question meant I was questioning my wife's account of the events that took place, and I didn't like the feeling I got from doing that.

I made the drive to Black Boy's house in twelve minutes and found him waiting for me next to his car.

"We gotta stop meeting like this," he said, smiling.

"Real funny, but this shit is serious."

"Kick it to me live," he said climbing into my passenger seat.

I ran down my visit with old man Doug and the conversation we had, watching his facial expression to see how he really felt. Of course he was a veteran street nigga, so he didn't give shit away.

"Text messages, huh?"

"That's what he said, and he also gave me the name of a nigga he said I needed to talk to."

"Who's that?"

"Robert Cook," I replied.

This time his response was visible because his eyes narrowed and he was studying me carefully. "You sure that was the name he gave you?" he asked.

"Yeah, but it seems like you heard it before."

"It just so happens that I have. You remember me telling you I didn't think it was no nigga from around here that dropped the hammer on your people, especially not with the money you were putting out for info? So, I started looking for out-of-town shooters who weren't picky about the work if the money was right, and that name came up. It came up again when I sent somebody to have a little chat with Aaron."

"By chat, you mean?"

"He spent a few weeks in the infirmary, but I couldn't send him home without getting my inside connect jammed up. He definitely living on borrowed time, though."

"What did you find out about Robert Cook?" I asked.

"Park your car and I'll fill you in."

I did like I was told and we got out and went inside his house. Black Boy didn't sell dope out of this house, but he lived in it like it was the trap. We walked into a wide-open space that should've been a furnished living room, but instead it was just dingy carpet with two bitched curled up in sleeping bags on the floor. We walked past the kitchen and dining room, moving to the bedroom at the very back of the house.

"I'ma warn you now, it stinks in this muthafucka," he said before opening the door.

The first thing I noticed was the wall-to-wall plastic, and sitting right in the middle of it was the remnants of a stocky black dude tied to a chair. The odor in the room was horrific. I could easily identify piss, shit, and burned flesh as heavy favorites in the combination. The man was covered in cuts and cigarette burns. His face was clearly deformed from a vicious beating, and from where I stood, I couldn't tell if he was breathing.

"Allow me to introduce you to Robert Cook," Black Boy said.

"Damn, bruh. Why you got a dead body in here?"

"Oh, he ain't dead. He just wishes he was. Ain't that right?" Black Boy asked, throwing a punishing left hook that threatened to tip the chair over with him in it.

"I gotta give it to him, though: he's a bad muthafucka because he ain't gave up no info. Yet."

It was hard to believe someone could take that kind of torture and stay silent. It was even harder to believe there was more Black Boy could do to convince him to talk.

"Maybe he doesn't know shit," I said.

"You know it ain't no such thing as coincidence, bruh, and his name done came up too many times. I got just what he needs, though," he said, sliding open the closet door a few feet away from the barely-conscious man. He reached in, pulled out some jumper cables, and walked around to stand in front of his victim.

"I want you to listen carefully, Robert. These cables are hooked to a generator in my closet, and I'm about to hook them to your dick and flip the switch. So, you wanna talk now or later?"

In an obvious struggle, the man raised his head high enough to look Black Boy in the eye, and he shook his head slowly.

"Let's party, then," Black Boy said, going back to the closet and turning on the generator.

There was no way I could be in the room for what was about to happen, and I made it back to the living room just as the first screams started. I didn't know what was crazier, the shit going on in the back room or the fact the bitches asleep on the floor hadn't budged. The screams lasted for a few minutes, and then Black Boy reappeared, going to the kitchen.

"Forgot the adrenaline," he said, coming back out with a small vial and needle.

For the next several hours I heard the kind of screams you could never forget, no matter how hard you tried. And then there was silence.

"Come here, Ahmani," Black Boy called out.

I steeled myself as best I could and went back in the room. I tried not to look, but the dude's dick looked like a dog's chew toy, and there was no doubt of the pain he was in.

"Speak, nigga," Black Boy commanded.

"I shot. I shot that car up. I-I was paid to."

"Who paid you?" I asked.

"K-K-Katrina Hudson."

Chapter Eighteen

"Bullshit," I said, taking a step toward him.

If Black Boy hadn't held up his hand to stop me, I probably would've got on the dude's ass for lying on my wife.

"It's-It's true, I swear. P-Paid me a $100,000 cash, plus travel c-costs. Rush job, flew me in the day before and t-told me to wait for her c-call. Didn't know there were kids in the car."

"Why the fuck did you shoot it up once you saw them?" I screamed.

"J-Just business," he replied.

My mind was absolutely spinning as I tried to make sense out of some shit that made no goddamn sense! Why would Katrina sic a hitman on my family? There was nothing to be gained from that except destroying me, and she had no reason to hate me that much. Why would she have married me and done everything else she had if she hated me? This muthafucka had to be full of shit. I opened my mouth to say just that when Aaron Charles' warning about Katrina needing to be the most important person in my world popped into my mind. This couldn't be about that, though, could it? No, no. No, because that would mean my wife was Charles Manson, Ted Bundy-type crazy.

"That nigga's lying, Black."

"Nah, my nigga, he ain't. You know that when it comes to getting answers, I do this shit, and it took a while to break him. I'm sorry, bruh, but he's telling the truth."

For a moment I simply stared at Black Boy, looking him straight in the eyes in search of any signs of deception on his part. Not finding any brought me a pain I wasn't ready for, along with enough guilt to carry me to the bottom of the ocean and trap me there.

"H-He's telling the truth?" I whispered, finally losing my battle against the tears rolling down my face.

Black Boy reached behind him and pulled a long-barreled .357 Smith and Wesson from his pants, checked it, and handed it to me. The weight of it in my hands was as heavy as my heart, and I knew even if I pulled the trigger, only one of those two things would get any lighter. To his credit, Robert didn't beg or plead when I put the gun to his forehead, but I'm sure that's because in his line of work he knew how useless that was.

"Just business," I said.

And then I pulled the trigger, decorating the wall and part of the closet door with the remains of his final thoughts.

Handing the pistol back to Black Boy, I turned around and stumbled from the room as the entirety of what his dying declaration meant hit me. My wife, the woman I'd promised the rest of my life to, was single-handedly responsible for destroying my world. It was hard to accept that, but not as hard as it was to think about what I had to do next.

"Hold up, bruh. Where you going?" Black Boy asked, following me into the living room.

"I-I'm going home."

"You want me to ride with you?"

"No. I gotta do this on my own," I said, walking out of the house and into the dusk.

The entire day had passed in one torturous scream that was still echoing in my head, but I no longer knew if it was mine or the man I'd just executed. When I got to the car, I checked my phone, finding several missed calls and text messages from Katrina and two calls from Elyse. As much as I wanted to go home and deal with Katrina, I still needed a minute to compose myself, and I needed to talk to someone.

I dialed Elyse's number and listened to it ring six times before I hung up and called right back. I didn't get an answer the second time, either, which probably meant she was taking a nap, but it only took a moment's debate before I decided to just show up on her doorstep.

For both emotional and practical reasons, we'd decided it was best if she moved out of my mom's place and into my old apartment. It made more sense than paying two rents, and there was a storage facility literally around the corner from my apartment complex for us to store all my family's belongings. Neither of us had the heart to get rid of anything, and we'd decided even if my mom wouldn't know her first grandbaby, he would definitely know her.

Thinking about my mom brought more tears because I'd been so wrong and so blind about Katrina. I couldn't see past our past to listen to her sage advice, and now I'd have to take that regret with me to my grave. How was I supposed to live with myself now that I knew the truth? The death of my mother, sister, and brother were my fault. Their blood was on my hands. Me continuing to live life didn't make sense, and it didn't seem fair. I tried calling Elyse again as I started the car, needing to hear her voice in the worst way. It rang three times, and then it was answered.

"So, you can call this bitch back, but you can't find the time to do the same for me?"

"K-Katrina?" I asked, feeling my heart come to a screeching stop in my chest.

"You sound shocked, sweetheart. Kinda how I was when I picked up this whore's phone and saw it was you who was blowing her shit up."

"What the fuck are you doing there?"

"If you would've answered your phone, dear, you would've known our baby was coming."

"Bitch, if you hurt my son —"

"Bitch? Did you just call me a bitch, Ahmani? That's how the fuck you talk to me, after all I've done for you?"

"I know exactly what you've done," I blurted out, regretting my words the instant they were spoken. Now was not the time to get into this conversation.

"What does that mean, Ahmani? What do you think you know?"

"Where's Elyse? Are you two at the hospital yet?"

"Don't answer a question with a question!"

"We can talk about this later, goddamn it. Now where is the mother of my child?" I yelled, feeling a tsunami of panic and fear consume me.

"I am the mother of your child," she replied right before the line went dead.

I already had the car moving as I tried calling right back. When I got no answer from Elyse's phone, I started calling Katrina's phone back-to-back, willing her through sheer force of brainpower to answer and be reasonable. Of course, that didn't work. I had no idea what Katrina meant by her last comment, but whatever she was up to wouldn't be going down under the watchful eyes of hospital staff. So, where was she? She couldn't force Elyse to move without a gun, and I knew she owned plenty of them. But if Elyse was in labor, she couldn't be moved. Logical deduction said they had to be at my apartment, so I pointed the car in that direction and pushed the engine to its limits.

My mind was racing, not knowing what I was walking into, but with each mile that passed I came to terms with one undeniable fact: Katrina was out of her damn mind! I had to accept that and face it, but at the same time I knew I couldn't control crazy, so I had to come up with some type of plan.

"Keep it simple, stupid," I said to myself, calling her number again.

There was still no answer on either phone, but I was minutes away. I may not have known what to expect, but I did know Elyse and the baby would need help, so I called 911 and explained the facts. There was no doubt in my mind I sounded like a hysterical madman. I just hoped they didn't think this was some type of prank call.

I skidded to a stop in front of my building and hopped out before the engine could stop roaring, praying I wasn't too late. Under any other circumstances I would've had my gun on me, but since my day had started with a trip to the jail, I had left it at home. It didn't matter, though, because if I had to give my life for my son's, I would without hesitation. I ran down the hill and around to the back of the building where my balcony was.

Just like I'd hoped, the shades were open and I could see into my living room, but what I saw defied logic and had my blood on ice. Hopping the balcony railing, I crashed through the balcony door, not caring about the shattered glass or the cuts I got.

"Give me my-my son," I demanded, struggling to my feet, and trying not to vomit from the heavy smell of blood in the air.

On the floor in front of the couch was Elyse, her chest just barely rising and falling in the dim lamplight. She was completely naked, making the gruesome incision down the middle of her stomach that much more obvious and horrifying. It looked like Katrina had cut her open and pulled my little boy out, leaving Elyse on the floor as discarded as the placenta and the umbilical cord. And if that sight wasn't enough, Katrina sitting on the couch, rocking my wailing son in her arms while trying to breastfeed him put the icing on the cake.

"I'm trying to feed him so he'll stop crying," she replied calmly.

"Katrina, you can't feed him because you're not producing milk."

"I can, too, feed him! I'm his mother, and a mother has the right to breastfeed her child anywhere."

"Katrina, please, just give him to me," I said, trying to sound calm and reasonable despite the stark terror that wanted to take over my entire being.

"I can't do that."

"W-why not?"

"Because if I give him to you, you're gonna leave. I know you're gonna leave me."

"Baby, I'm not gonna leave you. I'll never leave you. I just wanna take our son to the hospital and get him checked out to make sure he's okay," I said.

"He's fine. He's just hungry. And I know you're lying about leaving me. I'm not stupid, Ahmani."

"Baby, I —"

"Shut up!" she yelled, finally looking at me.

Her raising her voice only made the baby cry harder, and the look in her eyes made me want to cry. She was as beautiful as I'd ever seen her, wearing a light blue strapless sundress, but her eyes were diluted with madness.

"Katrina, I love you," I said softly.

"You did love me. I know you loved me, but you don't see none of that would've been possible with your mom around. I know she didn't like me, and it only would've taken a little more time for her to turn you against me. I only did it because I love you, Ahmani. I've always loved you."

I struggled to find words that wouldn't come out in a screaming tirade of profanity because I didn't wanna escalate the situation, but it wasn't easy.

"I know you love me, baby. And it wouldn't have mattered what anyone's opinion of our relationship was because I only wanted to be with you."

"Is that why you fucked this bitch after we were together? Don't bother lying, because she literally spilled her guts about everything."

"It didn't mean anything, baby. I —"

"I sacrificed for you. I gave you everything you could ever want and need, but that still wasn't enough, huh? I saved your life even though you weren't supposed to go down for my parents' murder. They didn't appreciate me, either. Bet they're rethinking that decision," she said, laughing.

As more and more was revealed, I realized my earlier assessment had to be re-evaluated, because this bitch wasn't crazy. Whatever she was, it was brand new on the market, and she was the founding daughter of the movement. The only way I could see out was to convince her I was on her side.

"No matter what's happened, baby, I still love you," I said.

"You still love me?"

"Yes, I do."

"Even though I had your family killed and I killed my own parents?"

"L-like you said, all we got is us," I replied, hating the taste of those words leaving my mouth.

"That's all I wanted, Ahmani. Since that night you saved me, I just wanted to be yours, and for you to be mine. And it was beautiful, babe. But I know it can't be that way anymore," she said, gently laying my son across the couch with his tiny little head almost dangling off the edge.

He was still crying in a very pissed-off way, but he appeared to be otherwise unharmed. I thought some sliver of good sense was taking over her brainwaves.

Until I saw the machete she'd kept hidden behind her.

"Katrina."

"Don't. Take. Another. Step," she said slowly, gripping the weapon with purpose. "You say you love me, and all we got is us, right?" she asked.

"R-right."

"Then the only child we should have should be ours. How can I look at him and not see you fucking his mother?"

"Katrina, please. I don't love her. We can raise him as our own, and you can be his mother," I pleaded.

"It won't work, Ahmani. You love him more than me already, and I refuse to share your love with anyone to that extent. Not *anyone*, Ahmani!" she emphasized. "Get it in your head, bae: you belong to me!"

"Katrina, don't!"

"It's for the best," she said, raising the blade high in the air.

Suddenly the lights went out, throwing the room into complete darkness, and my son stopped crying.

"No!" I cried.

To Be Continued...
Bae Belongs to Me 2
Coming Soon

Stay Connected with Us!

Text **LOCKDOWN** to 22828 to stay up-to-date with new releases, sneak peaks, contests and more…

Thank you!

<u>Coming Soon from Lock Down Publications/Ca$h Presents</u>

BOW DOWN TO MY GANGSTA

By **Ca$h & Jamaica**

TORN BETWEEN TWO

By **Coffee**

CUM FOR ME **III**

By **Ca$h & Company**

BLOOD OF A BOSS **IV**

By **Askari**

BRIDE OF A HUSTLA **III**

By **Destiny Skai**

WHEN A GOOD GIRL GOES BAD **II**

By **Adrienne**

LOVE & CHASIN' PAPER **II**

By **Qay Crockett**

THE HEART OF A GANGSTA **II**

By **Jerry Jackson**

TO DIE IN VAIN **II**

By **ASAD**

THE BOSS MAN'S DAUGHTERS **III**

BAE BELONGS TO ME **II**

By **Aryanna**

UNBREAK MY HEART

By **Misty Holt**

A DOPEBOY'S PRAYER **II**

By **Eddie "Wolf" Lee**

<u>**Available Now**</u>

(CLICK TO PURCHASE)

<u>RESTRAING ORDER **I & II**</u>

By **CA$H & Coffee**

<u>LOVE KNOWS NO BOUNDARIES **I II & III**</u>

By **Coffee**

<u>LAY IT DOWN **I & II**</u>

<u>LAST OF A DYING BREED</u>

By **Jamaica**

<u>PUSH IT TO THE LIMIT</u>

By **Bre' Hayes**

<u>BLOOD OF A BOSS **I II & III**</u>

By **Askari**

<u>THE STREETS BLEED MURDER **I, II & III**</u>

<u>THE HEART OF A GANGSTA</u>

By **Jerry Jackson**

<u>CUM FOR ME</u>

CUM FOR ME 2

An **LDP Erotica Collaboration**

BRIDE OF A HUSTLA **I & II**

By **Destiny Skai**

WHEN A GOOD GIRL GOES BAD

By **Adrienne**

A GANGSTER'S REVENGE **I II III & IV**

THE BOSS MAN'S DAUGHTERS

THE BOSS MAN'S DAUGHTERS **II**

A SAVAGE LOVE **I & II**

By **Aryanna**

A DOPEBOY'S PRAYER

By **Eddie "Wolf" Lee**

WHAT ABOUT US **I & II**

NEVER LOVE AGAIN

THUG ADDICTION

By **Kim Kaye**

THE KING CARTEL **I, II & III**

By **Frank Gresham**

THESE NIGGAS AIN'T LOYAL **I, II & III**

By **Nikki Tee**

GANGSTA SHYT **I II &III**

By **CATO**

THE ULTIMATE BETRAYAL

By **Phoenix**

DON'T FU#K WITH MY HEART **I & II**

By **Linnea**

BOSS'N UP **I & II**

By **Royal Nicole**

I LOVE YOU TO DEATH

By Destiny J

I RIDE FOR MY HITTA

I STILL RIDE FOR MY HITTA

By **Misty Holt**

LOVE & CHASIN' PAPER

By **Qay Crockett**

TO DIE IN VAIN

By **ASAD**

BOOKS BY LDP'S CEO, CA$H
(CLICK TO PURCHASE)

TRUST IN NO MAN

TRUST IN NO MAN 2

TRUST IN NO MAN 3

BONDED BY BLOOD

SHORTY GOT A THUG

THUGS CRY

THUGS CRY 2

TRUST NO BITCH

TRUST NO BITCH 2

TRUST NO BITCH 3

TIL MY CASKET DROPS

RESTRAINING ORDER

RESTRAINING ORDER 2

IN LOVE WITH A CONVICT

Coming Soon

THUGS CRY 3

BONDED BY BLOOD 2

BOW DOWN TO MY GANGSTA

Aryanna